DEATH

IN A

FAR

COUNTRY

DEATH IN A FAR COUNTRY

SHEILA MACGILL-CALLAHAN

St. Martin's Press
New York

Design by Lynn Newmark

Library of Congress Cataloging-in-Publication Data

MacGill-Callahan, Sheila.
    Death in a far country / Sheila MacGill-Callahan.
        p. cm.
    "A Thomas Dunne book."
    ISBN 0-312-09892-8
    1. Retired teachers—New York (N.Y.)—Fiction.   2. Americans—Ireland—Fiction.   I. Title.
PS3563.A29825D4   1993
813'.54—dc20   93-11465
                                                         CIP

First Edition: October 1993

10 9 8 7 6 5 4 3 2 1

For Leo

Acknowledgments

Many thanks to Daniel Tubridy, the owner of Pier 92 in Rockaway Park, for the many happy hours I have spent in his great restaurant; to Susan Cohen, my agent at Writers House; and to Barbara Follansbee, who told me I could do it. And thanks to my sisters, Patricia McGowan and Christine Mac-Gill, for diligent proofreading and editorial suggestions.

I

HE SANG BENEATH his breath, "Let the mountains skip with gladness, and the joyous valleys ring . . ." Brian MacMorrough Donodio slowed in his joyous lope down East Fortieth Street and briefly considered skipping mountains. Did they rise from the plain on gargantuan legs? Or did they content themselves with a more sober shimmy, bringing down rocks and trees on the heads of the luckless mortals who were witness to their giant joy? Anyroad, he knew how they felt. His feet traced a brief pattern on the concrete evocative, he hoped, of a roistering Rocky, an ambient Alp.

Then he caught the eye of the blue-shirted, black-holstered guardian of public sobriety who watched from the intersection. He straightened his features, pushed his horn-rims sedately up on the bridge of his nose, and resumed his loping progress. It would never do for a respectable, three-piece-suited, retired history teacher to be arrested in his wing-tipped Florsheims and carried off to wherever he would be carried off. No way. He would be late for his lecture. And how would he explain matters to Maire? His wife was a model of matronality—or a lascivious lassie, depending which side of the bedroom door she happened to be on. On which side she happened to be? No matter, he knew what he meant. A Manhattan hoosegow would definitely fall on the wrong side of the door.

And why this festal joy? This exuberance? (Latin root *uber*, his scholar's mind noted. Abundance. Fertility.) Because he had been bored since retirement. Bored, bored, bored. Maledictions on the cretins at the Prendergast School who decreed a shelf life of sixty-five. No matter how sweetened with CD, IRA, social security, and pension, retirement was the devil's work.

Now students waited for him at the Irish Historical and Cultural Center. Why had he mooched around the house for six months before listening to his daughter, who worked there part time, and offering to teach a course at this blessed place? Aha, here we are—a three-storied double brownstone, just shabby enough to be comfortable. He opened the door and went in.

There was no one in the hall, but a mighty thumping of drums and scraping of fiddles came from a room on the right. He cracked the door cautiously, not wishing to disturb whatever revel was in progress.

A youthful, sweating group was striving to master the intricacies of the six-handed reel and stumbling all over their feet in the process. One lady lacked a partner. Why not? he thought. In my youth I could foot a reel in Rockaway with the best of them.

He jettisoned his briefcase and hopped nimbly into the set, bowing to his partner and swinging her merrily about. "Oh, the bodhrans bang and the fiddles scrape, / Watch out for your toes, the west's awake," he warbled in approximate time and tune.

The music stopped. He bowed gallantly to his partner. She was striking, not pretty—striking. Hair, red on the sides, green on top, flowing every which way across her skull. Green eyes to go with the red hair, heavy black liner around them. A knife of a nose and a big, happy mouth. He sniffed delicately. He liked her perfume.

2

"You dance like an angel. Who are you?"

"Dr. Donodio. And you?"

"My name is Melisande Costello," came the answer in pure Ulster tones.

"You're kidding. Nobody's name is Melisande."

Her mouth turned down at the corners and the safety pin in her right earlobe quivered.

"Sorry, Melisande. It's a beautiful name. Some of my best friends are Melisandes. Now, will you be kinder than I deserve and tell me where the office or whatever is?"

"The whatever is on the second floor. One flight up and down the hall, first door on your right."

"And what is this?"

"We're supposed to be learning Irish dances. Why don't you teach a dance class? You're real neat."

Nothing is calculated to cheer a retired history teacher more than being told he is "neat." With a light heart Brian headed to the door, deftly sidestepping an earnest, big-bosomed lady with a whistle. She had a light in her eye he recognized. This was the dancing teacher, and she was determined to, one, find out who he was, and, two, corral him to help her teach.

He followed Melisande's directions. Up the stairs, down the hall. He could hear the hum of voices from behind many doors. This place was a hive, a warren, a maze. And somewhere was his own little cell. First door on the right. He tapped gently and eased it open.

A puffy-looking fellow was perched on the edge of a desk, phone cupped to his ear, leg swinging. He waved his free hand and pointed to a chair. The springs squeaked and Brian's sitting raised a waft of dust from the space around the cushion. A good-size office, pictures all over the walls, a threadbare carpet on the floor, furnishings circa 1934, a bookcase along one wall, and, incongruously, a computer terminal winking and blinking. He relaxed and eavesdropped unashamedly.

"No, we don't get green cards for people. . . . No, you

3

don't have to be a member to come to a lecture. . . . Sure, we'd like to have you join. We want everyone to join. . . . We have theater, classes in Irish history . . ." Brian sat a little straighter and touched the knot of his tie. "Look, I have someone in my office. Come on Wednesday if you're interested. Good-bye." He put down the phone.

"Sorry about that. What may I do for you?" He plunked into the oak swivel chair behind the desk.

Brian looked him over. There was something about the fellow he distrusted. A bit flushed about the eyes and the nose. He sniffed but could catch no trace of drink. A drinker's face though, if he'd ever seen one. His graying hair swept back from his forehead in sculptured waves, razor cut and blow-dried. His nose overhung a long upper lip that was curved back in a smile that did not touch his eyes, showing tobacco-stained teeth. The lower lip was full. His real chin was weak, propped up by another, false one curling below it. If he shed the fifty or so extra pounds he was carrying, his face would look remarkably like an animated pear.

He thought, Maybe I'm just jealous of all that hair being wasted on a face that even his mother must have had a hard time loving. His hand moved up to smooth his own sparse locks.

"I'm Brian Donodio. I'm supposed to be teaching a course in Irish history."

"Dr. Donodio, a pleasure. You'd be Deirdre's father."

"Guilty as charged."

"A lovely girl." He licked his lower lip and a hot light glowed in his eyes. Brian felt his hackles rise. "She's been a great help since she's started working here part time. I only wish we had enough in the budget to have her on full. I'm Barney Finucane." He half rose from his seat and extended a moist hand across the desk. "For my sins I'm known as the director of this establishment."

"It seems a fine place to me." And I'll be keeping an eye on you, he added to himself. He looked at his watch. "Maybe

4

we'll talk later about other things I can do to help besides teach."

Finucane reached to a rack behind the desk. "You have twenty students. This folder has the roll and we put in any announcements we want made." He looked. "I see someone has already left you a note."

Twenty heads turned as they entered the classroom. Brian reacted ecstatically to the smell of chalk and paper; he was home and fell naturally into the teaching manner honed by forty years' experience.

"I'm Brian MacMorrough Donodio. In case you're wondering how I came by a name like Brian MacMorrough Donodio, my father, God rest him, was of Italian ancestry, my mother a MacMorrough from County Meath. I'm a bowl of stew from the melting pot.

"Tonight we start a course in the history of Ireland. The land of saints and scholars, of Black and Tans, IRA and Orangemen, of Provos and Loyalists. And let us not forget the joker in today's deck, the wild, elusive green card . . ."

An hour later he was finished and shuffling his papers together when he remembered the note in his folder. He read and his brows rose.

"Anyone here named Maureen Sullivan?"

A few turned to shake their heads. Nobody answered.

2

THE ALARM WENT off at 6:30. Brian shot out a sleepy arm and slammed down the snooze button. Five more minutes. He slithered his shoulders down to just the right spot under the blanket, closed his eyes, and tried to relax into the delicious state between sleeping and waking. But he didn't quite achieve it this morning. He could feel the damn clock's inexorable digital face relentlessly pacing off the seconds, flipping over the minutes. Before it sounded again he slammed the off button and swung his legs over the side of the bed, his feet guided by subliminal radar into his sheepskin slippers.

Once he overcame his initial reluctance, early was his favorite time. He glanced at Maire, peaceful on her pillow, the slackness of sleep making her look older. After a shower and the fitness exercises mandated by uxorial tyranny, he padded down the stairs to the quiet kitchen.

While coffee brewed he let himself out the back into the garden. The house was Maire's, but the garden was his. Had been since the day nearly forty years ago when they'd proudly taken GI mortgage possession on the quiet Woodside street.

Antonio Seamus was then just a hopeful bulge under Maire's skirt; three months later Brian came home from the hospital and planted a pear tree in Antonio's honor. It was in full leaf now, as were the other trees. A peach for Kieran, plum for Maria, and cherry for Deirdre. In pride of place was Maire's apple tree. That had been there when they moved in, the sole remnant of some farmer's orchard.

The wading pool he'd built was a lily pond now, well stocked with proud golden carp, shaded by his grape arbor. He flicked out the few weeds that dared to show their heads between his immaculate rows, then switched on the sprinklers so the vegetables could drink well before the heat of the day. Yes, he could be proud of his garden, just as Maire was of the house. When they could have afforded something more pretentious, they never even considered it; too much of their life was tied here. When fire claimed the house on one side, they added that lot and, later, the lot on the other side. Now his garden was included on tours and he turned down more lecture dates than he accepted.

The house had been a real challenge. The postwar housing shortage had them sleeping in Maire's parents' living room. With the baby imminent they would have settled for a shack in Staten Island. The ramshackle warren of tiny rooms covered with depressing green siding had seemed like heaven. It was Brian's uncle who had tipped them off.

Everyone had been telling them not to buy, the place was a wreck. Uncle Luciano had been a carpenter in the old country. While all the others were clicking their tongues at cracked plaster and water-stained ceilings, he had wandered around the basement and attic, poking and peering, humming happily.

"Good house. Fine bargain. Buy it," was his verdict.

He showed them the heavy, hand-hewn oak beams and the pegged construction at least two centuries old. His eye traced for them the Dutch Colonial farmhouse hidden under the siding and jerry-built additions.

The restoration had taken years. Now the house nestled

in Brian's garden, silvery gray with white-and-black trim, its wide veranda facing the street. Researching the restoration had sparked Maire's consuming interest in interior design.

From inside the house came the faint "ping" announcing coffee. The best cup of the day. He went to sip in peace at the scrubbed deal table.

He wanted to sort out his impressions of last night's class while they were still fresh. What a queer, mixed bag they were. A few were easy to place. Two old men and one old woman who nodded off comfortably as soon as he started the lecture. Probably lived alone in furnished rooms and liked somewhere to come of an evening. The lectures were free and there was tea and Irish soda bread afterward downstairs. Nine who really wanted to learn. The usual smart-ass who tried to trip him up on minutiae to show he knew more than the teacher. Half a dozen boys and girls who thought this might be a promising place to meet the opposite sex. Good luck to them.

One man really intrigued him. Youngish, not more than thirty-five, named Patrick Garrity. Brian sipped at his coffee. He couldn't figure out why he was in the course. If he was not very much mistaken, the man knew more Irish history than he. He could tell by the way he listened, the cock of his head, the look of irritation at a particularly stupid question. Brian added him to the list of queries niggling his mind. Maire always told him he was too nosy for his own good.

"You should have been a policeman like your father before you," she intoned when he was particularly curious. "A detective, not a teacher. You'd have been as happy as a hog in a mud wallow."

And now he had a puzzle. Probably nothing, but fun to think about. He went to his study and got out the note.

Dr. Donodio:
   I'm a friend of Deirdre's. She says you're good to talk to, and I have to talk to someone. If you

8

can, meet me tomorrow morning at 10. I'm at Apt.
6C, 239 W. 22nd St. Please, I need help.

Maureen Sullivan

There was no Maureen Sullivan in his class and Information
yielded no telephone listing.

The clock said 7:30. He'd tried to call Deirdre's apartment
last night but there was no answer. He'd try again at eight,
though he seemed to recall Maire saying something about
their daughter being away for a few days. He remembered
when he was a very new teacher getting a similar plea from
a failing student. When he got to her house, her parents were
out. She'd opened the door in a see-through nightie. Of
course, he'd had all his hair then. He grinned at the memory.
He'd never told Maire.

He didn't have to worry about that sort of thing these
days. This time he'd tell Maire before he went. Better still,
he'd take her with him. If she wanted to come, that is.

For the first time since he retired, he was a happy man.
He had students, he had his garden, he had a puzzle. Two
puzzles. He'd make breakfast in bed for Maire and tell her all
about it. What should he make?

In the kitchen, the innards of the refrigerator glared back
at him. White, chilly, ordered. Eggs, that was it. A three-
minute egg, toast, bacon. He put the egg on to boil, slammed
down the toaster. The bacon? Ah, yes. Maire used the microwave. Five minutes full power? He glowed with satisfaction
at his culinary aptitude and wandered out to the garden to
pick flowers for her tray.

Flowers in hand, he glanced at the roses. A few looked a
little blown. He wandered over and nipped with his seca-
teurs. A cabbage caught his eye. It looked chewed. That was
the only word for it. Chewed. If he didn't look out, this place
would be turning into coney island. He'd have to check the
fence. The garden had to be perfect for Maire's fete on Sunday for St. Enda's. On hands and knees he started round the
perimeter. Aha! Right here! This is the spot . . .

"Brian!"

Oh my gosh, Maire's breakfast! He jumped up, knocking his glasses so they hung from one ear, and galloped into the kitchen.

Maire was standing in the middle of the room, arms akimbo, her white hair still ruffled from sleep. She glared up at him, a banty hen confronting a giraffe.

"I thought the house was on fire, but I might have known."

Brian looked around. The egg had exploded all over the stove and the bacon was charcoal strips. The toaster had decided to be temperamental and not pop. It always popped for Maire. "I was making you breakfast in bed." He proffered the flowers. "Here."

Her eyes twinkled. "How often do I have to tell you? Inside the house is mine, outside is yours. Sit down and I'll have breakfast on in a jiffy." She bustled around, setting things straight. "Tell me about last night. I'm sorry I was asleep when you got in."

He told her, ending with, "Do you think I should go over to see this Maureen Sullivan?"

"Well, there's no use trying to reach Deirdre. She's in Boston for some sort of training on the new Morrison visa regulations. She's staying there for the weekend. Here, get this inside you." She set an omelet under his nose and poured fresh coffee. "I think you should go see her. The poor thing may be in trouble of some sort, and if Deirdre told her to ask you for help, it may be something to do with that case she's working undercover on at the Irish center. Besides, you'll never stop fretting about it if you don't."

He mumbled through a mouthful of egg, "Want to come with me?"

"No, I don't think so. A man your age doesn't need a chaperone."

"That's what you think, woman." He caught her round the waist and delivered an eggy kiss.

10

"Go on with you now, that's enough of that. You know, it does my heart good to see you like this."

"Like what?"

"So happy. You've been like a cat rubbed the wrong way since you retired."

"Speaking of cats . . ."

"Yes?"

"Isn't it time for a new one?"

"A kitchen needs a cat, but somehow I haven't had the heart since poor old Smith had to be put down."

Brian left the house at 9:00, in plenty of time to walk to the subway. He hated driving and gladly relinquished the wheel to Maire at every opportunity. For him a car was an animate monster, one that growled, stalled, and made ominous noises. For Maire it hummed, purred, and glided. Better by far to leave these things to initiates in the arcane mysteries of the internal combustion engine.

Trust Deirdre to be away when he needed her, he mused as the train left the elevated structure and plunged into the bowels of the earth. He waited for the slight popping in his ears that signaled they were beneath the East River. He'd read that the tunnels were through bedrock, putting a ceiling between him and the silt on the river bottom, but he always felt a slight prickle at the back of his neck. He knew that someday the tube would rupture and the mud would come pouring in.

He shifted to the downtown Broadway local at Times Square. When he emerged at Twenty-third Street the sky was dark with the heavy stillness that precedes a storm. He had only about a block to walk.

He was fifteen minutes early. The house did not inspire confidence. A run-down tenement with an unlocked front door of smeared glass backed by a filthy net curtain. The three steps up from the sidewalk were chipped and uneven. They had not known the lick of the paintbrush in years. The

11

interior looked like a cave, the gloom barely pierced by a tiny bulb hanging unshaded from a wire. The walls were the tobacco-spit brownish yellow that only New York landlords obtain from God knows where. Certainly Brian had never seen it in any paint store. Sherwin-Williams would have turned up their toes and died of shame. Underfoot was a pocked tile floor, each ceramic octagon sharply edged in the black of ages.

And the smells. Brian considered himself a nose man. He had declared himself such in college locker room days just to be different, and that had started him cultivating his smeller. Now his educated proboscis wrinkled fastidiously. Cheap disinfectant predominated; beneath was the sourness of vomit, the ammoniac tang of urine, with an overlay of burning herb or hay, the only way he could verbalize the reek of pot. Merciful God, he thought, I hope this Maureen Sullivan is a strong woman.

The wiring hung loose above the doorbells. Brian looked doubtfully at the stairs; 6C must be on the top floor. Go home, said a cautious little voice in his head. "Ah, the hell with it," he answered himself aloud and started up the stairs at a run. By the second floor he was trotting, by the third he was plodding, on the fourth he pulled himself up with the bannister, on the fifth he halted out of breath. As he toiled up to the sixth floor he was muttering, "It had better be good, Maureen, or you'll hear the rough edge of my tongue."

He knocked. There was no answer. He knocked again, then laid his hand on the knob and pushed. The door swung in silently.

"Maureen."

No reply.

Louder, "Maureen Sullivan?"

The silence rolled back. Filtering up from the street he could hear traffic, the wail of a siren. Here, on the sixth floor, the noises only underlined the hush. Then he heard a curious buzzing.

"Don't be getting fancies," he told himself just for the

comfort of hearing a voice. She's out. She'll be back any minute. Go in, write her a note, and leave. His feet did not seem to be obeying his head. Go on. He forced himself forward a step. She'll come in through that door any minute and be angry I let myself in. He pushed forward another step. Down the little hall he went, the buzzing hum leading him on, getting louder and louder.

"Maureen, Maureen. It's Brian Donodio, Deirdre's father."

No answer.

The hall opened into a small, white-painted living room, the walls gay with posters. The old board floor was stained dark red. A few cheap Indian rag rugs. Not much furniture. A couple of big cushions, a table with two chairs, a studio couch. The flies were everywhere. Beating against the window, clustered in a dark cloud on the ceiling, jostling, pushing, fighting for position around the studio couch against the wall. A dreadful smell, overlaid with another odor he had smelled before. He couldn't place it, but it was at odds with this shabby room.

She was lying on the couch. She might have been asleep, but for the smell and the flies gathered thickly for their obscene feast. It was not until he stood over her and forced himself to look that he saw the rosary twined through her folded hands, crossed around the knife driven deep into her heart. His stomach heaved as he forced himself to touch her marble wrist. He lurched to the window and threw it open, then covered her face with his handkerchief. The elusive smell had thickened and was strong around her, sickeningly at odds with the awful smells of death. Where had he smelled it before?

At the foot of the couch sat a marmalade cat, its eyes staring, its tail fluffed into a club, its fur a nimbus. A low, continuous growl came from its throat. He held out a comforting hand. "Hello, Smith." Claws flashed, missing his

13

snatched-back hand by a hair. The cat flattened to impossible thinness and slid under the couch.

On the end table the phone shrilled to life. Still caught in a haze of unbelief, he lifted the receiver.

"Hello."

A man's voice. "Who's this?"

"Brian Donodio. And you are . . . ?"

The click of a broken connection.

Feeling stupid, he took a deep breath and dialed 911.

3

WITHIN TEN MINUTES the uniforms came charging up the stairs. Brian met them in the hall. He pointed wordlessly in the direction of the living room. He could not even be sure that the dead woman was Maureen Sullivan. She might turn up at any moment. He was tempted to say nothing of the note, at least until he had a chance to speak with Deirdre. But if he withheld it, how could he explain his finding of the body? He could feel his father, the cop, breathing down his neck. "Don't do it, son," the old man was saying. "Answer whatever they ask to the best of your ability."

"Okay, Dad," he muttered guiltily.

There was a light touch on his elbow. One of the uniforms. "May I have your name and address, sir?"

Brian complied.

"And can you identify the victim?"

"No. I've never seen her before."

The man cocked an eyebrow. "Then, how come . . ."

Brian interrupted him. "Officer, could I sit down?" He decided that the time had come to be a frail old codger. "It's been quite a shock."

"I don't see any harm in that. There's a stool in the

kitchen. Just don't disturb anything. I've sent for the detectives, they should be here any minute."

"May I call my wife?"

"Let's wait for the detectives."

"Of course."

Brian found that he had not lied. When he slumped onto the stool he was shaking from head to foot and sweat was pouring off his forehead. For a minute he wallowed in self-pity. Nothing in his existence had prepared him for this. Then, from some deep well never before tapped, anger rose and flooded his body. For the first time in his life, emotion and object were in perfect harmony, uncolored by selfishness, vanity, lust, or greed. That girl had not deserved to die, whatever she'd done. He'd find the bastard if the police didn't and make him pay. If she *was* Maureen Sullivan, she'd asked him for help and he'd been too late. If she was someone else, she was somehow mixed up with Maureen . . .

"Excuse me, Mr. Donodio?"

The man standing in the doorway was young, with the gold shield of a detective pinned to his jacket. His dark hair tumbled over a tanned face with regular, but not memorable, features. In fact, he looked like any young New York businessman in a light-weight gray suit and blue shirt. Only someone who was very observant would catch the faint bulge of the gun in his shoulder holster. He smelled vaguely lemony, with overtones of saddle soap. Brian decided he liked him.

"I'm Donodio. And you?"

"Detective Connolly. Suppose you tell me about it."

Brian made up his mind. "It started with this note." He handed over the much-handled piece of paper. At the end of his story he added, "The 'Deirdre' in the note is my daughter. She's a field agent with the Immigration and Naturalization Service. She'll be in Boston till Sunday."

They were interrupted by one of the detectives. "Sarge, take a look at this." He was holding out a wallet and a green

16

passport. Connolly flipped them open and his eyebrows rose in questioning arcs as his lips pursed in a whistle.

"Well, I'll be damned."

"I hope not," said Brian politely.

"By the picture on her passport, she's your Maureen Sullivan. And get this. She's a cop."

"A cop?"

"Here's her card." He was looking at the wallet as if mesmerized. "Ban Garda Maureen Sullivan."

"I don't get it."

"You mean to tell me, Mr. Donodio, that you didn't know the victim was a member of the Garda Siochana, the police force in the Irish Republic?"

"I've told you everything I know." Even to his own ears Brian's story sounded improbable. He could just imagine what it sounded like to Connolly.

"While we're waiting for the medical examiner and the lab crew to finish up, would you mind telling me again about your movements last night."

"What do you mean? You can't think that I . . ."

"So far I don't think anything. We have to wait for the autopsy, but the Doc says about twelve to fifteen hours. You say that you taught a class last night at the Irish Historical and Cultural Center. You are referring to that place on East Fortieth Street?"

"That's right."

Step by step Connolly led him again through the previous evening. "What time did you say you left?"

"About nine-thirty. My lecture was from eight to nine, then I stopped downstairs for a cup of tea."

"What time did you get home?"

"About ten-thirty."

"Can anyone vouch for that?"

Brian's heart sank. "No. My wife was asleep when I came in."

"So you could have gotten home at any time."

"I could have, but I didn't. I got home around ten-thirty."

17

Connolly stood up. "I'm going to ask you to come to the station to make a statement"—he waved the note—"especially about this. Wait here in the kitchen. If anything else occurs to you, we can discuss it at the station."

"Except . . ." He aimed the last word at Connolly's retreating backside.

"Yes?"

"May I call my wife; and what's going to happen to the cat?"

"ASPCA I guess. Unless a claimant turns up."

"Could I take it home?"

"I don't see why not, if the beast doesn't belong to someone."

"Could this have something to do with a case of my daughter's?"

Connolly whistled impatiently through his teeth. "Now, how should I know. Your guess is as good as mine. We'll check. Now, Mr. Donodio, do me a big favor and just wait. You may call your wife from the station."

Left to himself, Brian looked around. A scrawny plant on the windowsill was putting up a game struggle against the lack of sun and the stale air coming in through the air shaft. Some kind of kalanchoe hybrid by the look of it, but he didn't recognize the variety. The plastic species wand was sticking up in the pot. "Bonanza Mikkel Kalanchoe," it read, "propagation prohibited." Despite his shock at the murder, Brian chuckled. How the hell did you make a plant understand that it had to practice birth control? Did you bear down on the bees? Or maybe you just let the poor thing wither and die without sun or water, so it had no inclination to bring little kalanchoes into the world. He slipped the pot into a paper bag lying on the counter; maybe he could sneak it home to sunshine and good soil on Maire's kitchen windowsill.

There was a soft brush against his legs, a plaintive meow. Smith looked up at him, amber eyes slitted. She—now her coat was flat and normal he was able to determine gender—

18

walked over to an empty saucer by the sink, reached out a delicate paw, and scraped it across the floor.

"I'm hungry. I'm thirsty. Get off your haunches, human, and attend to me," she announced in a voice that could not be gainsaid.

Brian explored. He found a can of tuna in the cupboard and a can opener. The noise attracted the officer in the next room.

"What the hell do you think you're doing?"

Brian fixed him with the glare that had reduced many an impudent student to shambling, shuffling confusion. "I do not think I am doing anything, young man. I know I am feeding a hungry cat." He cast a satisfied glance at Smith, who was crouched neatly over the can, tail wrapped snugly round her paws, tucking into the tuna with a single-minded devotion to life's essentials. "Do you have some difficulty with that?"

"The sarge won't like it."

"Let me worry about him. I'll tell him you came in too late to stop me."

Connolly's voice came from the front room. "Okay, that wraps it up." Out of the corner of his eye Brian saw two men wheeling out a gurney with a long, plastic-shrouded shape. He crossed himself and murmured, "Eternal rest grant unto her, O Lord." His eyes rested on the uniform cap of the young officer, who flushed and whipped it off.

Connolly stuck his head around the door. "We're ready to go now."

"What about her?"

"Hell, I forgot about the cat. We'll have to take her down to the station and call the ASPCA from there."

"I'll carry her." Brian scooped her up, pleased that she sensed his friendship and did not struggle. With his other hand he reached for the bag with the kalanchoe.

"What's that?"

"A kalanchoe."

"A what?"

19

"A plant. I'd like to see it propagate."

Connolly's eyebrows rose and he shook his head.

The ride to the station was a subdued affair, the rain a gloomy counterpoint to the violence of murder. Despite his anger and alarm, Brian had hoped for a ride in a blue and white with the siren whooping and lights flashing. Instead he got a sedate progress in an unmarked car that punctiliously obeyed all traffic regulations. Brian petted and soothed Smith while he tried to think of something appropriate to break the oppressive silence from the front seat.

"Aren't you supposed to read me my rights?" he ventured.

"What for?"

"I thought . . ."

"Mr. Donodio, you are not under arrest. You are coming to the station for questioning and to make a statement. If you feel you need legal counsel, you will be given the opportunity to call a lawyer. We are a long way from making an arrest."

Brian probed the response for a scintilla of comfort. Finding none, he scratched Smith under her chin and tried to get his thoughts in order. He had two courses open to him. He could make a statement and bow out, or he could make his statement and deal himself a hand. Sherlock Donodio? He knew what he should do, what Maire would want him to do. He settled back in the seat. He would do his level best to find Maureen's murderer, either by helping the police or, if they got nowhere, on his own.

4

AGENT DEIRDRE DONODIO of the U.S. Immigration and Naturalization Service slumped in her chair. There was boredom, she decided, and then there was terminal boredom. She checked her watch. In another fifteen minutes she would slip over into terminal boredom. Her left little toe was itching deep in the crack between it and the next one. She wiggled and slid it round her shoe but could get no purchase on the itch. One of life's uncelebrated pleasures was the scratching of itches.

The man on the platform droned on. He was citing the dire consequences to employers who failed to file an I-9 form. Deirdre made another dutiful attempt to listen. It was the third and last day of the conference and her mind was running on other things.

She had arranged two days of her annual leave so she could stay through the weekend in Boston. One of the Boston agents had offered to show her around. She thought about him for a moment. A chauvinist, but at least tall enough. Dark and hairy, a bit like King Kong.

She thought of herself as resembling an amiable giraffe. She sketched a giraffe with long, blond hair walking hoof in paw with a gorilla. He might be fun for the odd weekend. Damn. Her toe was itching again.

She eased her shoe all the way off and scratched luxuriously. She'd really have to do something about the celebration of scratching. Let's see . . .

> There was a young man from Siberia
> Who had a most itchy posterior.
> He said, "I have ants
> In the seat of my pants . . ."

Interior, inferior, drearier . . . Her search for a rhyme was interrupted by the lecturer.

"Agent Donodio, if you can spare us a moment."

She could feel the blood surging into her face. Why did she blush so easily? "I'm sorry, could you repeat the question?"

"Of course." His voice was long-suffering. "All I asked was . . ." He broke off as the door of the room opened to admit one of the clerks from the outside office. "What is it? We're in the middle of a conference."

"I'm sorry, Mr. Pilbeam." The woman's voice was soft but it had a peculiar carrying quality. "There's an urgent call from New York for Agent Donodio."

Deirdre eyed the clerk gratefully. She had never before seen a sudden angel in bifocals and polyester double knit. She slipped on her shoe and stood up.

"I'm sorry to have to miss the rest of your lecture, Mr. Pilbeam. It's been very interesting." She beamed at her fellow victims as she turned to follow Polyester wherever she chose to lead.

"Take the call at my desk. It's the one over by the window. Just push the button on line three."

"Thanks. And thanks for getting me out when you did. I don't think I could have stood it for another second."

A big grin broke over Polyester's face, displaying teeth of military straightness and unnatural brightness. "He's an

22

awful windbag, isn't he? Get to your call now, or the man will get tired of holding."

"Agent Donodio speaking."

"Sergeant Connolly, NYPD. Sorry to interrupt your conference. What can you tell me about Maureen Sullivan?"

"Is something wrong?"

"She's dead, Ms. Donodio."

Dead! She had liked Maureen, felt they might become friends. A spate of questions rose to her lips, but her training asserted itself.

"What precinct are you calling from?"

"Manhattan South. Homicide."

Homicide. Then it wasn't an accident. "I'll call you back."

She scrabbled hastily in her pocketbook for her notebook with its handy list of New York police numbers. While she listened to the tinny electronic beeps bridging Boston and Manhattan, Maureen's face formed itself in her mind. They had stopped for coffee Monday night after a lecture at the center. The redhead had sat quietly in the booth, staring across the table until Deirdre shifted uncomfortably under her gaze.

"I shouldn't be staring at you. I'm sorry."

"Is something the matter, Maureen?"

"If only I knew who to trust here in New York."

"Manhattan South, Officer Gibbs speaking," a woman's voice sounded in her ear.

"Sergeant Connolly, please. This is Agent Donodio of the INS."

"Hold on a minute."

"Now do you believe I am who I say I am?" Connolly growled.

"I never doubted it for a minute. You'd have done the same."

"Sure I would. Now what about Maureen Sullivan?"

"I tried to call her last night, but there was no answer. I had told her to expect my call."

"What time was that?"

23

"About eleven-thirty."

"The ME sets the time of death around eleven, so that fits. What were you calling her about?"

"She was worried but wouldn't tell me why. I met her at the Irish Cultural Center. I liked her a lot."

"We'll get back to that later. You sitting down? I have another surprise for you."

"I'm sitting. What is it? Your technique's a real spellbinder."

"You know a man named Brian Donodio?"

"He's my dad. What does he have to do with this?"

"He discovered the victim."

Deirdre's stomach gave a peculiar, empty heave. She had quit smoking six months ago, but now she felt the need. Polyester's pack and lighter were lying on the desk. She caught her eye and motioned to the pack. At the woman's nod, she lit up. One puff convinced her she had quit for good. It tasted like a mouthful of camel dung. How did Dad come into this? Her voice followed her thought.

"How did he happen to do that?"

"Just what I was going to ask you."

"What did he say?"

"Come on, you know better than to ask a question like that."

"Yeah, I do. And I'm not going to talk any more about it over the phone. Where is my dad now?"

"Here. At the station."

"What's he doing there? Is he charged with anything?" Her voice was rising in pitch. "Has he got a lawyer?"

"Relax. He's making a statement is all. We're waiting for it to be typed."

"Let me speak to him."

"Nothing easier. He's sitting right here by my desk."

"Hello."

"Dad, what have you been up to?"

"I'm fine, dear. Sergeant Connolly here tells me that I'm

24

not allowed to discuss the case with you or he'll take the phone away from me."

Deirdre felt the tension in her shoulders relax. She chuckled. "I'd like to see him try. I know who'd come off second best in that encounter."

"We won't put it to the test. I just wanted you to know I was all right and not to worry. I must say I'm very impressed with Sergeant Connolly and very distressed by today's events. I still have to tell your mother."

Deirdre made up her mind. The hell with the weekend with the gorilla. "Dad, I'm coming home. I won't spend the weekend in Boston and I don't want to talk any more right now to Connolly. By the time he calls back, I'll have left. Tell him I'll be on the next shuttle. I left my car at LaGuardia, so I'll come straight to the house. 'Bye."

She grabbed her purse and made for the door, stopping for only an instant to say to Polyester, "Thanks a million. If he calls back, I've gone."

5

LATER, ON THE plane, Deirdre sat back and tried to think about Maureen, but she could only give her half of her attention. The other half was in the cockpit with the pilot, making sure that the plane stayed safely in the air where it belonged. On the footrest her right foot was firmly on the gas, left on the brake. Deep down she was sure that if she relaxed her vigilance for one moment the 4:30 shuttle would land on its keister in Boston Harbor, tearing down the tattered ensign on Old Ironsides and generally playing havoc with all the up-market, down-market, and middle-market types around Faneuil Hall.

She willed relaxation and forced herself to concentrate on Maureen. What did she really know about her? Nothing solid, but she had taken to her immediately. They had met maybe five times. Deirdre had given her a quick tour of New York—Rockefeller Center, St. Pat's, Fifth Avenue. Down the subway to South Ferry to see the harbor and ride to Staten Island, squinting at Lady Liberty in passage. Then on to South Street Seaport.

One thing she had noticed. Maureen's eyes, like hers, were never still. Their bodies assumed the same defensive stance. Police training showed in her every action. She spoke before she thought.

"Are you a cop?"

She could sense Maureen's withdrawal. "Now why would you think a thing like that, I wonder?"

"Something about the way you look around, the way you react to a crowd. My grandfather was a cop and he had the same way about him. Look, let's not discuss it now. We'll find a place where we can sit and have a drink."

The bar at the Polaris Pub was elbow to elbow with trendy Wall Streeters, but the dining room was blessedly empty in the middle of the afternoon. Deirdre steered Maureen to a table and they sat in uneasy silence, broken only by the ordering of drinks.

Maureen was the first to speak. "Are you a policewoman, then?"

"No. When I was a kid my dad and I had a game of trying to figure out what people do from the way they act. I still play it. And you?"

"I'm nothing so important." A hot flush rose under her freckles; lying came hard to this woman. "I'm just a civil servant."

Deirdre did not press her. Instinct told her that, whatever her problem, Maureen would not be party to an immigration scam. To fill the silence she pointed to the noisy crowd gathered around the bar. "Look at that bunch of fools out there lapping up the booze; and every one of them mortgaged up to the eyeballs."

Maureen settled back and took a deep swallow. "We have characters like that at home, too. Every place has them. In fact . . ." She paused and looked a little uncertain.

"What is it?"

"Don't be offended, now. I was just going to say I was surprised there are so few of that type here in the States. At home we have the idea that the Yanks are all like that crowd in there."

Deirdre grinned appreciatively. "You should meet my

27

dad. I think the two of you would get along famously. He's a great man when you're in a spot. He's going to be teaching a class down at the center."

The conversation drifted on from one desultory topic to another, the constraint between them thick as clotted cream ever since she'd asked if Maureen was a cop. It was Maureen who made the move.

"Thanks for a lovely day, but I have to run along. I promised to meet someone at about half past six and it's almost that now. Will I be seeing you Monday at the center?"

"I'll be there. I had fun today. I always enjoy showing New York off to visitors."

They parted. Monday night was the last time Deirdre had seen her.

The plane swooped low over Queens Boulevard. Moments later the wheels touched, hopped, and touched again. Deirdre glanced out at terra firma regained, eased the pressure of her foot on the footrest, and relaxed her shoulders. She had done it again, brought the old 4:30 safely home. The other passengers, ignorant of their debt to her, were already crowding the aisles, pushing to be the first off the plane. When the aisle cleared she grabbed her bag and made a quick dash to the parking lot.

6

SERGEANT CONNOLLY PERCHED uneasily on the edge of the couch facing the fireplace. He was more impressed than he would admit by the spare, clean lines of the Dutch Colonial farmhouse nestled in its luxurious garden. The living room centered on an immense stone fireplace, filled for the summer with a luxuriant Boston fern.

Over the mantel hung an Irish landscape he was sure was a Yeats original. Parquet, mellow from years of waxing (no polyurethane here), showed around the edges of the Aubusson rug. The furnishings were an eclectic mix, many with the unmistakable glow of cherished heirlooms.

Across the wide hall that ran the length of the house was the dining room. The Sheraton table and chairs gleamed softly in the afternoon sun that drew rainbow glints from the small Waterford chandelier. Books were everywhere, lining the central hallway, on both sides of the fireplace, tucked under the bay window in the dining room. And they were only the overflow. On the drive to Woodside Brian had mentioned his study and library. Connolly shook his head. This was definitely not your average Queens family.

He had driven Brian and the cat home. Smith, an upwardly mobile feline, had accepted her improved position with aplomb. She sat on the hearth to the manor born, preening her whiskers with a graceful paw, yellow eyes fixed balefully on him. He heard the slam of a car door and the voiceş of Maire and Brian raised in a confused babble.

He half rose to join them, then settled back. It was a touchy situation. They had put Brian in one of the interrogation rooms at the station and, to be perfectly honest, were bearing down a little on him. Not that they had anything on him, it was just that he was all they had. Connolly had not known what to make of him. He sat there without turning a hair, telling a story so unbelievable as to be laughable. Connolly finally believed him simply because it had to be true. The man was too intelligent to invent such a load of cod's wallop (as his mother used to say).

He had played the part of the rough cop. Brian sat back in the suspect's chair and crossed his legs. "Sergeant Connolly, I'm getting sick of this sophomoric attempt to intimidate me. It won't work, you know."

Connolly felt like a kid caught in the boys' room with a marking pen at the ready, although he really hadn't done much in the way of intimidation. Just growling and looming a bit.

"I have nothing to be intimidated about." Brian rose and walked to the door. "I suggest that either you charge me with something and book me, in which case I'll contact my lawyer, or . . ."

"Or what?"

"We sit down like two civilized men and discuss things. My father, God rest him, who retired from the department as a captain, would have chosen the latter."

"Who was your father, then?"

"Antonio Donodio."

Connolly drew a deep breath. Though the old man was thirty years retired and long dead, he was still a legend in police circles. "Why didn't you say so, Mr. Donodio?"

"Why should I?" Brian retorted snappishly. "I did not

know I had to flaunt a relationship to be treated with courtesy. And while we're at it, I'm *Dr.* Donodio. Now, I have nothing to add to what I have already told you. Unless you wish to make a fool of yourself and book me, I'm walking out this door and going home. My wife will be getting worried and it's long past my lunchtime."

"Please stay." It was a different Connolly. "I'm sorry, sir, I thought . . ."

"You thought I was an old man you could push around. Well, I'm not." There was a hint of softening in his manner. "Tell you what, Sergeant, I'm sorry I lost my temper. I'll call my wife. You try to get hold of Deirdre in Boston. And why don't you send one of your men out for a sandwich for me. Corned beef on rye with mustard would be just the ticket. Then we'll have a good talk."

Connolly opened his mouth to assert his authority. What came out was, "Would you like coffee with that?"

Brian, good humor fully restored, twinkled at him, "Tea with lemon, and be sure the water's boiling."

Connolly wrenched his mind back from the humiliation of it all. While they waited for the sandwiches he used the time to make a quick visit to the captain. Captain Mendez's reaction was immediate. "Donodio's son," he barked, "every courtesy. Keep me informed."

Now he had to deal with Deirdre Donodio. From what he had gathered on the phone, she was as independent as her old man. He had orders to work with her and it was awkward meeting on her home territory. He strained to hear the conversation, but the tones were guarded. He pictured her to himself. Ms. five by five with a little mustache, that's what she'd sounded like on the phone. He didn't think women should be cops, anyway.

The door opened on the three, but he had eyes only for one. A quote slipped into his mind. It had been under his sister's picture in her high school yearbook, and they had teased her with it ever after. "A daughter of the gods, divinely

31

tall and most divinely fair." There she stood, someone for whom the tag was not a joke.

He leaped to his feet, trying to achieve a single fluid motion, a coiled steel litheness. His knee caught the edge of the coffee table, upending it and sending a vase flying. He made a frantic grab, bending double, rear aloft. The silence was shattered by a tearing pop of stitches as his pants, tight as befits the macho image, split stem to stern.

The family Donodio choreographed to a halt. Maire was a lady. Her lips twitched only once as an expression of polite concern spread across her face. Brian guffawed and yelled, "You'd better sit down, man. At a time like this, discretion is more precious than manners."

A delighted expression spread over the face of the goddess. She whooped, struggled for control, lost it, and whooped again. Between whoops she gasped out, "Sergeant Connolly, you're wonderful. I wouldn't have missed this for the world."

Maire took charge. "Now, it could happen to anyone; you mustn't feel badly. Brian, give him a pair of your pants to change into and I'll have these stitched in a jiffy. Stop your nonsense, Deirdre. Can't you see the poor man is embarrassed?"

Connolly arose, hand clutching his gluteus. Led by Brian, he shuffled crabwise around Deirdre and back down the hall, his fire red face turning a dangerous shade of puce as he heard Deirdre howl again with helpless laughter.

When he returned with a pair of Brian's sweats flopping around his ankles, Deirdre was striving for businesslike self-possession.

"I checked with my office while you were occupied. It seems we are to cooperate on this one but you'll have to do all the overt stuff, since I'm undercover at the center."

"That's right, Ms. Donodio."

"For heaven's sake, call me Deirdre. I think we're on a first-name basis by now. What's your name? I can't call you Sergeant or Mr. Connolly."

32

"My friends call me Con."

"Good enough. Let's go out in the garden while Mom fixes your pants. You two can fill me in and Dad can show off his pride and joy."

"I doubt if I'll appreciate it properly. I'm a real Manhattan native and not into gardens. Somehow all the other boroughs feel like foreign parts to me." He stood on the back steps and looked over the glowing tapestry of flowers and trees, herbs, and vegetables that Brian had sown over the brown earth of Queens. "I must say, though, this is totally beautiful."

"And only eighteen minutes from Grand Central. Let's go sit in the arbor. You passed, you had the right reaction. Dad can give you the grand tour later."

"The problem is," Brian remarked as he seated them under the canopy of light green grape leaves that trembled slightly in the early evening breeze, picking up and shattering gleams from the westering sun, "we have been discovered by the real estate mavens. We are, God help us, being gentrified—or we were until the housing market went soft, thanks to the gang of thieves in Washington. Whoever coined that abomination of a word deserves to have his ears pinned to a copy of the OED. We'll be showing off a little on Sunday. Maire is running an open house to show off her interiors; it's called 'To Grandmother's House We Go.' The proceeds will benefit the immigration program at St. Enda's."

Deirdre interrupted. "Let's get down to business. I know you've told it all to Con, but tell me again in your own words what happened today. I'll interrupt when I have questions."

Con was not listening. Did she have a boyfriend? A fiancé? Her ring finger was comfortingly bare. A significant other? She had her own apartment. Did she share it? Oh, hell, did she have a lover? A woman like Deirdre had to have a lover. He felt a stirring, a quickening catch and glanced down in horror at his lap. Damned sweats show everything. He crossed his legs and pushed down. Ouch. He shifted uneasily and she cast a curious glance.

"Something you want to add?"

"No." He slipped his notebook to his lap as extra insurance and looked up to catch Brian surveying him with a knowing eye. Damn this family. To distract himself he tuned in on the conversation. Just in time.

"What do you think, Con?" Her voice was like a chime of bells.

He wrenched himself away from the contemplation of the curve of her nose. "I think we have to wait for the lab reports and to hear from Dublin. Anything we do now is theorizing ahead of data." His voice was purposely harsh and matter-of-fact.

"I think"—she held his eyes steadily—"that somehow it all centers in immigration and the Irish center."

"That's my gut feeling, too. But it could also be that she made a date with some guy, he turned out to be a nut, and that was that. No connection at all with anything you've been working on."

"Could be. I know she was meeting someone on Saturday night, but I don't know who." She filled them in on the details of their Saturday tour. "When we met at the center on Monday we went out for coffee afterward and she was a bit more forthcoming."

Con leaned forward eagerly. "Did she say who she met?"

"No." Deirdre's brow puckered with the effort of total recall. It had been social night at the center and, as usual, an informal *ceili*. Maureen had surprised Deirdre by singing several of the old songs. Later they had gone to a coffee shop across the street to have a quiet chat.

When they were settled in the booth Maureen seemed uneasy. "I wish I knew who to trust here in New York."

"Something wrong?"

"It's Monica, she's my younger sister."

Deirdre waited.

"She came to the States about six months ago. For a while she was writing and she called a few times, then nothing. It's

34

as though she dropped off the face of the earth. Telephone disconnected and the post office returning the letters."

Deirdre's scalp began to prickle. "Did she have a green card?"

"Not that she told us. First she told us she was coming on holiday, then she told Mum not to worry, she had the immigration all fixed. I checked with the U.S. authorities at home. They had no record of anything but a tourist visa. Anyroad, I came over here to find her."

"Where was she staying?"

"A place up in the Bronx on Bedford Park Boulevard. I went up there. The woman who rents the rooms remembered her. Said she moved out in a hurry one day. Didn't say where she was going. I'm afraid something's happened to her."

"I can understand that. Have you been to the police?"

"No. Monica's the type who gets caught up in things. While she was at university she got in with a radical group. I'm afraid she may be mixed up with something political. It would be like her to bite off more than she could chew."

Deirdre caught the waiter's eye and gestured for more coffee. "What are you going to do now?"

"I haven't decided. I'm staying at an apartment on Twenty-second Street. One of the fellows at the center said I could use it. He only stays there occasionally. It's a bit of a dump, but I'm running out of money and going round in circles. What should I do?"

"Who loaned you the apartment?"

"He asked me not to tell anyone. He's afraid everyone would want to start staying there if the word got around. I see his point." She folded her lips firmly.

"I think you should go to the police or the immigration. Anything could have happened." Deirdre wanted to insist, but the only way she could do that would blow her cover.

Maureen stood up and shrugged into her jacket. "You may be right. I have one other lead to follow. If that's a dead end, I might do just that."

While she was paying the check Deirdre said, "I have to go to Boston tomorrow for a meeting. Promise me that you'll talk to my dad if this lead doesn't pan out. He'll be teaching a course at the center starting on Tuesday." She scribbled on a leaf torn from her notebook. "This is his home number. I'll call you at eleven-thirty on Tuesday night to see how things are."

". . . and that was the last I saw of her," Deirdre finished. "Before I left for Boston I put Monica's name in the computer and it came up okay. As far as I could tell she's legal, but it's odd that Maureen claimed there was no Irish record. I've asked for all the paperwork."

"Well, that gives us something to go on," Con said. "Who loaned her the apartment? Where is Monica? Why is there no Irish record? Maureen must have checked through the Garda."

It was nearly midnight when Deirdre let herself into her apartment. Con had seemed willing to stay forever. He had the grand tour of the garden, made appreciative noises over Maire's dinner, and promised to be on hand for the open house. She'd felt his eyes on her the whole time but had not been able to catch him. It was after eleven when he stood up reluctantly.

"It's been a grand evening, but I'm on at eight o'clock tomorrow. Can you meet me at the station in the morning? We should have word from Dublin by then and the preliminary findings from the lab."

Their arrangements made, he left. Deirdre turned to meet the eyes of Maire and Brian.

"Not a word out of you two, okay?"

"Okay," Maire echoed.

"Whatever you say, daughter. Safe home."

She glanced round at her quiet, lamplit room. Usually she relished the aloneness. Tonight it just seemed lonely. When

36

she slid into bed she thought without regret of the Boston gorilla and her lost weekend. As she coasted into sleep a great stag came and stood by the blond giraffe. The two stood together as the gorilla waddled off into the sunset.

7

Brian held himself still in the bed. Just because he couldn't sleep was no reason to wake Maire. Over and over again his finding of the body played through his head. He had held it at bay all day, but now in the small hours it danced inexorably in the front of his mind. Again and again he mounted the squalid stairs, stepped through the quiet apartment, found the body . . . body . . . body. At 4:00 a.m. he gave up the struggle and went downstairs.

Two cups of coffee later he still couldn't turn off his internal tape. He put on jeans and a sweatshirt and went to mend the fence where the rabbits were getting to the cabbages. But New York never sleeps. Certainly New York's Finest proved they never did. Five minutes after he started work there was a screech of brakes and a head poked warily over the fence.

"Just what do you think you're doing?"

Brian was delighted with the interruption. "Mending a fence."

"At this hour of the morning?"

"Seemed as good a time as any. I couldn't sleep," he offered as extenuation.

"Well, watch it, sir. Are you going to be out here long?"

"Why?"

"It's not safe to be out here alone at this hour. You never know who's going to come by."

Brian surveyed his fence. "About another hour, I'd say."

"We'll drive by a couple of times."

"Very kind of you."

After they left he went to the kitchen and poured the rest of the coffee into a flask and built two roast beef sandwiches. He carried the tray out to the table and went on with his fencing.

Twenty minutes later the car stopped again. "Everything okay?"

"Everything's fine, gentlemen. Might I tempt you with coffee and a sandwich?" The eastern sky was just shading to dark gray.

"Don't tell the sarge."

"I wouldn't dream of it."

The younger officer headed straight for the food but the elder stopped and looked around. "I've often admired your place, Mr. . . . ?"

"Donodio. Brian Donodio. Kind of you to say so."

"I do a little gardening myself." He pointed. "May I ask you about these?"

Brian's eyes lit up. "The Michailovsky Fritillaria? They're a Turkish flower recently introduced to this country. Burpee started selling them about three years ago. You should come back and see them when they bloom."

"I go for roses, but I don't have room for very many. There are over twelve thousand varieties, you know."

Brian was charmed. A rose-growing policeman.

He led him to the table and settled him down to the serious business of eating. "Tell me, do you know a Sergeant Connolly? He works out of Manhattan South. Homicide."

"Con Connolly?"

"That's the one."

"Not to say know him," the younger man said round a mouthful of roast beef. "Know of him. Why?"

"Well, I found a body yesterday."

"No kidding? Whose?"

"The Irish Garda, Maureen Sullivan."

"Geez." The young cop's eyes got bigger. "And Connolly caught it?"

"And Connolly caught it." He'd been about to tell them about Deirdre but decided it might be unwise, since she was undercover. "Now do you see why I'm interested?"

The older man spoke up. "He's a good man, got a rep, and they put him on the sticky ones. By the way, I'm Chris Muldoon and this is Hank Wojakowski. Thanks for the refreshments, but we have to go."

Brian saw his mistake; Muldoon was turning wary. Wojakowski had more to say.

"Your daughter, sir, would she be that blond di . . . young lady I've seen going in and out here?"

"Wojakowski." There were ominous overtones in Muldoon's voice.

"Why, yes, that's Deirdre. I had no idea that you kept such a close eye on everyone."

A big grin spread over Wojakowski's face. "It's not hard to keep a close eye on a young lady like that, sir."

"I see. Well, she's a black belt and a champion marksman, or should I say marksperson? I'll give her your regards."

"I'd rather you gave her my phone number."

"Wojakowski!" The veins were bulging on Muldoon's forehead. "Take the rest of your sandwich with you, and come!"

"Sorry you have to go, gentlemen. Officer Muldoon, come over some day when you have time and I'll show you my roses. I have a few interesting varieties."

He'd learned a little. Connolly was smart, well thought of, a young man on the way up. That meant he'd bust a gut to solve the case. But he had one advantage over Con. People at the center would be more likely to talk freely to him, and he had a perfect reason for going there tomorrow as soon as they opened. Of course, no one knew Deirdre was with the INS, but he would talk to a different group than would confide in her.

Suddenly he was sleepy. He padded upstairs, stripped, and slid in beside Maire. The fence could wait. Sleep reached up from the pillow to grab him.

8

COLLEEN COP CROAKED, screamed the *New York Post*. IRISH EYES AREN'T SMILING, trumpeted the *Daily News*. IRISH POLICE OFFICER SLAIN, was the staid heading of *The New York Times* on page two of the Metropolitan Section under the centerfold.

> The body of Ban Garda Maureen Sullivan, an officer in the Garda (police) of the Irish Republic, was found yesterday in an apartment in the Chelsea section of Manhattan. Officer Sullivan had been killed by a single stab wound in the heart. Garda officials in Dublin stated that Officer Sullivan was not engaged in an investigation in New York. She was on her annual leave and had received an extension of time to take care of personal business. A representative of the New York City Police Department stated that the police have several leads, but no arrest is imminent.

He cracked his knuckles savagely. All of the questions about that damn little bitch Monica. His eyes focused for a minute on a patch of ground near the house. The weeds had grown up. He couldn't even be sure of the spot now. Or could he? One rectangle showed a lusher green. He'd have to do something about that. No. Best leave well enough alone. He was imagining things. But he wasn't imagining that fellow Donodio. He'd found her. What was he doing in that apartment? How much did he know? Why did this have to happen now? With all the new Morrison visas approved by Congress, it was time to quit. Another few weeks and all of the machinery would be in place, then no one could touch them.

He got up and went to the bathroom. This was his second shower of the morning. Funny how he couldn't seem to feel really clean lately. It was hot and humid, that's all. New York had a filthy climate. Why not shower as often as he wanted to keep comfortable?

He toweled himself and reached for the cologne.

9

BRIAN SAT IN the kitchen. He felt quivering, sensitive, as though the top layer of his skin had been peeled. *The New York Times* was propped against his coffee mug. He read and reread the story about Maureen Sullivan. Somehow, seeing it in print gave reality to yesterday's horror, took it out of the realm of vivid nightmare.

Smith pressed against his ankles, rubbing the scent glands in the sides of her face back and forth in an intricate pattern across Brian's trousers to proclaim to other felines that this particular human was marked as her property and no one else's. Smith now accepted the house as her right and proper domain, but she still cringed in terror when invited to partake of the larger delights of the garden. She leaped nimbly to Brian's lap and disposed herself, sheathed claws kneading his knees.

"Where do we go from here, Smith?" Brian's fingers found the perfect spot for stroking just behind her right ear. "You're all set unless the ASPCA calls in with a claimant. Are you a stray who moved in for a temporary handout? I'd love to know who loaned Maureen that apartment."

The phone rang. He answered quickly so as not to awaken Maire.

"Hello."

"Dad?"

"No, it's the archbishop of Canterbury. Who did you think it would be at this hour? Are you calling to lecture me, Deirdre?"

"Not lecture you. I just wanted to ask you not to go nosing around in Maureen's murder. Please promise you won't. It could be dangerous."

"Whatever gave you such an idea? I'm sure that you and Con will handle everything very efficiently between you."

"Well, just leave it to Con and me. You have enough to do with the open house on Sunday, and you're not fooling me any with that evasive answer."

"I hope, my dear, that your investigative talents are better than your syntax."

"Never mind my syntax." She sounded like the little girl who used to defy her older siblings. "I just can't have my father messing in one of my cases, even if he did find the victim. I'll look like a fool and it might even go on my record that I'm indiscreet, and that could end my career. Period. Full stop. And you might blow my cover. That could end my career very nastily. Please promise?"

"You've made your point, daughter. I won't "mess in," and if I hear anything down at the center I'll let you know. Fair enough?"

"Fair enough. Thanks, Dad. Talk to you later. I have to meet Con at the station at eight o'clock."

Brian sat back down and resumed his conversation with Smith. "Where were we, Smith? That apartment where I found you—whose is it? Let's make a list."

He reached for the pad and pencil next to his mug and started writing.

1. Who is the apartment rented to? Who owns Smith? Did the police turn up anything interesting when they searched?
2. Why did Maureen think I could help her? When did

45

she put her note into my class folder? Did anyone else have an opportunity to read the note? It was sealed, but does this mean anything?

3. What was the smell in the apartment?
4. Does the center have anything to do with anything? If so, what?
5. Why don't I like Barney Finucane?

He gazed at the list. This was all stuff the police would consider and handle better than he, and he had promised Deirdre. It was going to be hard to keep his promise and still find out who killed Maureen. A real exercise in casuistry. Well, he'd never disgraced his Jesuit education and was not going to start now. He fixed his gaze on Smith.

"Why can't you speak? Since you can't, we're just going to have to use the Socratic method. If I ask the right questions, the answers, always assuming that I get some and am not told to mind my own business, should lead to the cause. Do you agree?"

"Do I agree about what?" Maire inquired from behind his right ear.

"Ah, good morning, my love. The question was not addressed to you. Smith and I are having a colloquy."

"What you mean is you're trying out the arguments you are going to use on Deirdre so you can weasel your way into the Sullivan case."

Brian favored her with a look that was at once deeply guilty and totally outraged. "I'll have you know that I promised Deirdre only this morning that I wouldn't mess in, as she phrases it."

Maire sat opposite, cradling a mug of coffee. "And I'll bet you've spent the time since her call trying to think of a way round your promise without actually breaking it."

"Utter nonsense."

"Don't 'utter nonsense' me, Brian Donodio. I've known you for forty-two years, and I know when you're up to something. I'm going to be out all day and right into the

46

evening. I have a meeting in Manhattan today and then I'm going out to dinner, so you'll have to manage for yourself."

Brian grinned. He had forgotten that Friday was one of Maire's consulting days, though he certainly didn't quarrel with the whopping fees she earned as an interior designer and decorator. This meant he could nose around the center to his heart's content and no one the wiser. He beamed at her.

"Enjoy today, my dear. What sort of consultation are you doing?"

"A new client. This is just a preliminary meeting. I'll get the details when I meet with her. Now, I have a delivery this morning of things for the open house, and the decorators are coming. If you have time, would you help them clear out the furniture from the boys' room? See that our stuff isn't damaged when they carry it down to the basement. It's to be done over as a model "grandchild's room.""

Brian made a face. He was not big on furniture wrestling. However, *City Slicker* magazine was doing a feature on both the house and his garden. Maire had a genius for picking a theme. "To Grandmother's House We Go" had caught everyone's fancy. The AARP was sending in busloads of senior citizens (a euphemism he hated; why not call us "old folk"?). St. Enda's immigration committee was doing the refreshments and parking.

He gave Maire a dutiful peck and rolled up his sleeves. All of the important part of the investigation was going on without him.

The decorators were prompt and careful movers, transporting everything to the basement with a minimum of fuss. Maire had not stinted in getting a first-class crew. "All off the taxes," she'd airily informed him.

After clearing the rooms, they brushed the woodwork's pristine colonial green with villainous streaks of brown and gray until it gave the appearance of either not having been painted for years or having been assaulted by moppets urged to self-expression by a demented nursery school teacher.

47

When Brian protested he was told, "We have to get a country look. It'll wash off."

"It had better," he replied, surreptitiously rubbing at an unobtrusive spot with a moistened finger. It did.

Next the truck was unloaded and a woman arrived to supervise. She was definitely "now" in her Armani slacks and raw silk blouse. Slim, dark, and intense, about forty. Her hair rippled to her shoulders in a two-hundred-dollar cut, her briefcase was from Mark Cross.

Brian was grimy from shifting furniture to the basement. His jeans were spattered from old paint jobs and caked with dirt from last night's fence mending. The woman glanced at him and dismissed him.

"Who's in charge?"

"I am," Brian answered mildly.

"You?" Her eyebrows arched. She looked at the head decorator, a young man in designer jeans with a gold earring in his right ear, for confirmation. "Is he really in charge, Rene?"

Rene smiled gleefully. "You've put your foot in it this time, Kimberly. May I present Dr. Donodio, the householder, the man in charge of the garden part of the exhibit, and the husband of Maire Donodio. Who, by the way, will not be very happy with your gaffe. Dr. Donodio, the lady with the foot in her mouth is Kimberly Pettigrew, though I doubt if that's her real name any more than Ralph Lauren's is his."

Brian hated this sort of thing. He was gravely courteous. "A natural mistake, Ms. Pettigrew. I look like something the sanitation department would refuse to pick up in this outfit. Tell me"—he waved at the burgeoning heap of goods and chattels—"are these supposed to be the lares and penates of the Donodio household?"

She looked at him blankly. Brian sighed. What did they teach them in these schools?

"What I mean is, is this supposed to be the equipment of a present-day grandmother? It looks more like what my own grandmother, God rest her, might have had around the house, except I think my grandmother would have relegated most of this stuff to the attic, or gotten rid of it entirely." He pointed to a Windsor rocker covered with the ghosts of several different paint jobs and an old bench whose wood showed signs of dry rot.

Kimberly looked at him blankly. "This is what's big today."

He indicated the wooden doll house with its Victorian gingerbread trim and the rocking horse covered in real, slightly moth-eaten pony skin. "I seem to recall that my girls had a pastel monstrosity they loved called Barbie's Dream House and that the rocking horse was a big plastic fellow that bounced on springs. I think they're still in the basement. If I dug them out, wouldn't that make for a more truthful exhibit?"

He registered an incredulous stare but never heard her answer. The bell gave a long ring followed by an urgent tattoo, followed by another ring.

On the door step stood a young man, hand raised for a second fusillade.

"You're Brian Donodio." It sounded like an accusation.

Brian admitted that he was.

"I'm Sean Morrissey."

"I'm sorry, Mr. Morrissey, am I supposed to know you?"

"I was a friend of Maureen Sullivan."

Brian snapped to attention. He'd thought the fellow had something to do with "Grandmother's House." "Come in, Mr. Morrissey. Pay no attention to all these people. Let's go into my study, where we can talk in peace."

The man sat in the wing chair facing Brian. His shoulders were hunched and his huge hands worked spasmodically in his lap. "I . . . I don't know where to begin . . ."

"Try the beginning. What was your relationship to Maureen?"

His head snapped up. "Nothing like that. I know what you Yanks mean when you say 'relationship.' We had an understanding, you might say. I hadn't popped the question

49

yet, but we'd seen a lot of each other, and I knew that sooner or later . . ." His voice trailed off.

"So you were keeping company?" Brian used the old-fashioned phrase. He thought it would give the man confidence.

"That's it. Yes, we were walking out together in Dublin. Then I couldn't get work, so I thought I'd chance my luck here in the States. I'm a surveyor, but I'm just a construction worker here. But that's not important. What is important is, it's all my fault she's dead." He started hitting the arm of the chair.

"Pull yourself together, man, and tell me what you mean," Brian said sharply. "How is it your fault? Did you stab her?"

Morrissey jumped up and stood over Brian. His face was scarlet and a vein throbbed in his temple. "I could choke the life out of you myself for saying a thing like that. I loved her. It's only your age that keeps me back." He subsided into the chair and raised a haggard face. "God, I'm sorry. I don't know what's come over me. It's my fault because I should have been with her Tuesday night. It was me that put her note in your folder. I saw you Tuesday night at the center, but you didn't see me. Then I was supposed to go over to that dump on Twenty-second Street where Maureen was staying, but I didn't go."

Brian knew that he should stop him at this point and call Sergeant Connolly. He put the thought aside. If he did, he'd never hear the end of the story.

"Why didn't you go?" Deirdre's accusing face rose in his mind. He resolutely pushed it back.

"I can't . . . can't tell you more than that." The jaw pushed out belligerently.

He salved his conscience. "You should go to the police."

"I can't do that, either."

He took a shot in the dark. "You're not in the U.S. legally, are you?"

"What makes you say that?"

"Well, if you were you'd go to the police and tell them what you know, and I don't think you'd be here talking to me if you had any hand in what happened."

But even as he said this, he wondered if Morrissey's seeking him out might be part of some elaborate double bluff.

"Tell me, what was so important on Tuesday night that you broke your date with Maureen?"

"Fella out in Jersey called me about a job."

"What fellow?"

"What's that have to do with Maureen? Just a fella I know, that's all." He had the ivory skin and dark hair of the black Irish, but now his skin looked more gray than ivory. If he was guilty, he was the best actor Brian had ever seen. "What I want to know is, what are the police doing? You're the man that found her, you must know something."

Brian temporized. "It's still early, but you look as if you need a drink." He got up and poured a couple of fingers of single malt. "Here. I think your best course is to go to the police, but if you won't, there's nothing I can do about it. Can you tell me anything about what Maureen had discovered about her sister?"

Morrissey tossed off the drink and a little color returned to his face. "Thanks, I needed that. I know that she was afraid something bad had happened to Monica, but I don't know any more than that. We went out together on Saturday night. She told me then she was seeing someone Tuesday night who she hoped would help her find Monica."

"Did she tell you who?"

"No. She didn't know herself. Just that the fella who loaned her the flat was fixing a meeting for her. That's why she wanted me there. Said she needed a witness. But she didn't push it. I just thought it was Garda training made her say it." His eyes filled up and he fell silent, blinking to hold back the tears.

"Where can I get in touch with you?"

"No offense, now. It's not that I don't trust you, but I'd sooner not give you my address. Here——" He scribbled on a

51

slip of paper. "This is a pub up in the Bronx where they know me. If you want to be in touch, call this number and ask for Matthew. He'll get a message to me. Don't bother to get up, I can see myself out."

After the door closed behind him, Brian sat with his hand on the phone. On the one hand, he should call Con. On the other, what did he really have to tell him? Maybe he'd go up to the Bronx this afternoon and have a couple of drinks.

He salved his conscience by writing out a full account of the visit while his memory was fresh. He'd give it, along with the glass with Morrissey's fingerprints, to Con when he'd found out a bit more. Meanwhile, he'd check up on the boys and girl who were fixing up "Grandmother's House," then drop by the center to see what was going on there.

The decorating crew was gone. Brian looked gloomily at the transformed room with its streaky woodwork, old lace tablecloths draping the windows instead of proper curtains, and archaic toys. There was even a straw sailor hat hanging behind the door and a strange child's coat displayed on a rack. It was made of blue velvet and trimmed with fur. He dredged his crossword memory. By golly, it was a pelisse.

One thing was marvelous. Suspended from a hook in the ceiling was a model plane. A wonderful thing of balsa and tissue paper. Not one of the plastic monstrosities with snap-in parts with which today's deprived youngsters had to be satisfied. A big one, made from one of the expensive kits. He was ten years old again and Uncle Stefano, the glamorous uncle who was a captain in what was then the army air corps, had come to visit. He had presents for all, and Brian's was the model airplane kit that made him the envy of the block.

His father cleared a special place in the basement. For weeks he hurried home from school to hunch over the precious pieces, reading and rereading the flimsy instruction page until it ripped at the creases and his mother had mounted it between two panes of glass so he could see both sides.

Inch by inch the model had grown as he glued all of the

fidgety pieces of balsa together in strict order, his head swimming from the glue. They called it "dope" in those days and did not realize its potential for harm. Then the agonizing attachment of the tissue cover to the frame, knowing that a single rip would be failure. The painting. Then the final, persnickety gluing of the decals to the fuselage.

Oh, the sweetness, the triumph, the admiration of parents and siblings. The careful passage to school holding the treasure. And the awful moment when Hank Harris, the school bully, grabbed it from him and hurled it high into the air and it crashed into a fractured mess of wood and paper.

"Dumb plane's no good," Hank taunted. "It can't even fly."

With reverent hands, he eased the plane off its hook. It was the same model, the *Spirit of St. Louis.* He realized that tears were streaming down his cheeks.

10

It was after two o'clock when Brian got to the center and climbed to Barney Finucane's office on the second floor. The door was ajar. He gave a token brush of his knuckles and pushed it open. Finucane jerked upright in his chair with a startled exclamation. His right arm flashed out to sweep forward a pile of papers to cover the things in front of him. He was not fast enough. Brian caught a hurried glimpse of a straw, razor blade, and two lines of white powder neatly ordered on a small mirror. Dull red washed over Finucane's unlovely countenance, and the look he gave Brian was anything but genial.

He snapped, "We're not open yet."

"It's late," Brian observed mildly.

"B'God, you're right." The bonhomie of the professional Irishman slid on like a glove. "I lost track of the time entirely. What may I do for you?"

This was a good question. Brian realized he had only thought ahead to the interview, but not to how he could bring up the subject of Maureen and make it seem natural. For a minute his mind was a stubborn blank, then inspiration struck.

"On Tuesday I told you I'd like to do something more than just teach one class. I thought we might have a little chat about what else I can do."

"A man of your talents and learning, I'd have to give the matter some thought." He reached in his desk for a tissue to mop his streaming nose. Brian watched, fascinated. He had read that cocaine users sniffled when they needed a fix, but this was the first time he'd seen living proof. "Why don't we set up an appointment next week and talk about it?" He honked again. "These summer colds are terrible," he added as he rose from his chair ready to shake hands and wish him Godspeed.

Brian was not going to be brushed off so easily. He sat back firmly and ignored the outstretched hand. "We could do that, but I'd rather have a little chat here and now. But first, why don't you sniff up that muck on your desk that you hid when I walked in. Then you'll be comfortable."

The sweat stood out on Finucane's upper lip and forehead and his voice rose to the upper register. "I don't know what you mean, but," he added with weak belligerence, "it sounds damn insulting to me." Even as he spoke his hand was sliding over the papers concealing his fix, trying to gauge the damage.

"Sniff it up, man. Then we'll speak of many things." Brian's eyes sparkled inquisitively as Finucane carefully removed the papers. His fix was scattered across the face of the mirror but not dispersed amid the papers. He grabbed the blade and remarshaled it into two lines when Brian added, "Which of many things shall we speak about? How about Maureen Sullivan?"

The hand holding the blade jerked convulsively. "Have you no decency, man? Don't sit there watching me. This is a private matter." Brian averted his eyes and donned his men's room face. Silence seemed to stretch forever, but finally he heard two double sniffs and judged he could stop pretending to be dumb and blind.

Barney's eyes met his. "Mind you, this is not what you

think. It's a prescription the doctor gives me for a nervous condition."

"And I'm one of the Pygmy people from Borneo."

"Ah, Donodio, give a man a break, can't you. If the lace curtain biddies who are on the board of this place were to get word of my nervous complaint I'd be out on my arse before you could wink, with no pension. And it's not easy for a man my age to pick up a job."

Brian's heart felt a stroke of pity. He knew with bleak certainty that he was not cut out for this sort of probing and prying into another's weakness, particularly when it might have no bearing on Maureen's death. He sought refuge in the rational intellect's greatest invention, the justification.

"How you clear your sinuses is none of my business, Finucane, unless it has a bearing on Maureen Sullivan's murder. Did you know I found her body?"

"Jesus, Mary, and Joseph," he crossed himself. "God rest her soul, it's a terrible thing to happen. I came in early today myself to see the police."

"Is that so," Brian murmured. "And what did they want to know?"

"That's my business. If it's yours, you can ask them."

Brian remembered the way Con had loomed over him at the police station. He stood to loom a little over Barney. You're poking your nose in, his conscience said. No, I'm not. Shut up. All I'm doing is having a bit of a gossip. His conscience was right. He was looming very impressively and Barney was cowering back.

"So tell me about Maureen. What do you know about her?"

"Nothing, so help me. She came here about three weeks ago and was asking around if anyone knew her sister. Said she was looking for Monica Sullivan. I looked in our files, but we had no one by that name in the membership. And that's all I know. Why don't you sit down? You make me nervous standing over me like that."

Brian collapsed abruptly into a chair. He felt a bit of a

fool. He'd found only one new fact: Finucane was a coke sniffer. But did it tie in to Maureen's death?

"Tell me"—Brian sat further back in the chair and crossed his legs—"what are you doing here at the center about the immigration situation?"

"Mainly a few lectures on the changes in the law."

"In my parish in Woodside, St. Enda of Aran, we have a regular clinic twice a week where people can come with their problems. I could do that on Tuesday night before my class."

Finucane relaxed. He was on familiar ground. "I think I can guarantee that such an undertaking would be very welcome. I'll bring it up at the board meeting next week." He made a note on his calendar. "Now, is there anything else I can do for you?"

The terminal on Barney's desk was somehow hitched up to a telephone with a plastic thingamajig. Brian knew nothing of computers, but it looked like a fancy setup for a small outfit. Well, he was on a fishing expedition, so he might as well fish. He pointed to the gadget. "What's that thing hitched up to the phone for?"

Barney shot to his feet as though his tenderer parts had been caught in his zipper. "Get out of my office, you nosy bastard," he screamed. "That's none of your business. And don't show your face around here again."

"What about my class?"

"Never mind your class. I'll cancel it."

"What are you afraid of? Is that phone thing for the IRA? Or maybe you're running some sort of scam?"

"If you were a *real* Irishman you wouldn't even ask these questions. But what can a man expect from a fecking half Eyetalian?"

Brian rose to go. He certainly had drawn blood, though he wasn't sure what color. He added a parting shot, though he didn't know exactly what he meant by it. "Don't wrap yourself so tight in the green flag that you choke yourself."

He glanced at his watch as he left the room. Two-thirty.

57

He had four hours to kill before the first of the evening activities at the center. He was almost certain that Barney wouldn't dare cancel his class. He'd be too afraid Brian would complain to the "lace curtain biddies."

Well, for sure he couldn't go poking around now. Finucane might be moved to violence. Four hours gave him time enough to run up to the Bronx and look over that bar where they knew Morrissey.

A call to the number Sean Morrissey gave him yielded the name and address of the Four Green Fields on Tremont Avenue. His only excursions to the Bronx in recent years had been to the New York Botanical Gardens or scholarly colloquia at Fordham University, always by car. Since it was his invariable habit to stick his nose in a book and let Maire do the driving, he was not prepared for the damage done by years of wear and civic neglect. His brain told him that the tough-looking characters grasping paper-covered bottles were doubtless hardworking citizens going about their lawful pursuits. His brain told him that the boys and girls in skin-tight jeans and leather jackets with booming radios were blameless students en route to and from institutions of lower and higher learning. But his heart didn't believe it, and neither did his gut. He scrunched low in his seat, trying to look inconspicuous. He was the only rider in a business suit. By the time the train drew into the Tremont station he was positive that this had been a bad idea.

He remembered Tremont Avenue from his college days. A nice street lined with small businesses, a few neighborhood watering holes, a place where friends gathered on stoops for a couple of jars and the Friday night dances in the parishes were the highlights of the week for teenagers. A place where the cop on the beat could spot a stranger and find out his business without any outcry about civil rights. He was prepared for change, but what he saw in contrast to his mental overlay of the remembered street struck him like a blow.

Cheap stores spilled onto the sidewalk, cracked steps led up between the stores to tenements of unimaginable squalor. Ill-clad, dirty children. Why weren't they in school? His heart turned over at the sight of them as he wondered what chance they had.

The Four Green Fields was an oasis, freshly painted, with a green-and-white-striped awning. He stepped up to the bar with a feeling of relief.

"What will it be?"

"Pint of Guinness." He laid a bill on the bar. "I'm looking for Matthew."

The bartender laid down his change. "Which Matthew would you be looking for?"

Which indeed? "I'm really trying to get in touch with Sean Morrissey. He told me to leave a message for him here with Matthew."

The man's eyes narrowed suspiciously. "Sean Morrissey, is it? Now what do you want with him, I wonder?"

"That's my business."

"And who might you be?" The man's eyes shifted from right to left. His hands were under the bar. Brian smiled nervously. Detection seemed so easy in books. This was the point at which the intrepid shamus flashes a C-note and the bartender tells all. He had an uneasy feeling that if he tried it, the C-note would be stuffed down his throat.

"What's your name?" he asked the bartender.

"What's yours, if it comes to that. State your business or leave a note. If someone named Sean Morrissey comes in and asks for it, I'll see he gets it. But get this, mister, I don't like snoops, and I don't like guys in three-piece suits who come

60

in asking questions like the world owes them answers for the price of a pint." He turned his back and starting polishing a rack of spotless glasses.

Fine detective he was. He finished his pint and scooped up his change. Damned if he'd leave a tip. In the mirror behind the bar he saw the door open to admit a party of four. Two men and two women. Oh my God, one of the women was Deirdre! She plunked down on the stool next to him without a sideways glance and spoke to the bartender.

"It's a hot afternoon, Matty. I'll have a nice, cold Bud."

It was after six when he got back to the center. He poked his head around the door and into the lobby. No sign of Barney. More to the point, there was no immediate sign of Con.

He went first to the room where the dancing classes were held. Today there was no sweating group conscientiously discovering their roots. Only Melisande, his green-haired partner (Lord, was it only three nights ago?), moping in a corner, sniffling occasionally as she sorted out a pile of sheet music.

"Hello there."

"Hello." She did not even glance up. "No classes tonight."

"Melisande, it's me. Dr. Donodio." She looked up apathetically, her eyes red and swollen. "My dear, what's wrong? Is there anything I can do?"

"There's nothing anyone can do." She swiped the back of her hand under her dripping nose. "I'm upset about Maureen Sullivan."

"Did you know her very well?"

"No, but I knew her sister Monica. And Monica's disappeared, and now Maureen has been m . . . m . . . murdered." She drew out the last word in a long, upward-inflected stutter as though she could not believe this could happen to anyone she knew. "I heard you found Maureen?" She turned her swimming eyes up in question.

61

"Who told you that? Try to remember," Brian urged gently, "it could be very important."

"Oh, I don't know. Some fellow who was around earlier. What does it matter? Is it true?" Her eyes urged him on.

"It's true, but I can't talk about it. I promised the police."

She broke down entirely. "Why won't anyone tell me anything."

Brian drew her gently to her feet and pulled a large white linen handkerchief from his pocket and held it to her nose as if she were three years old. "Blow," he commanded firmly. Melisande blew. "That's better," he approved briskly. "Now we'll go over to the lounge and have a cup of tea and you'll tell me all about Monica and how you came to know her."

"But . . ."

"No buts, come along." He flung a bracing arm about her drooping shoulders.

When he opened the door of the lounge he found out what her "buts" were about. Con was seated behind a table with two uniforms, one to take notes and the other just in case. The latter rose to his feet and stood over them. Seated in the chair in front of the table was Barney Finucane, looking thoroughly miserable. Before Brian could say a word, Con beat him to the punch.

"Melisande, I thought we asked you to wait across the hall until we called you. Dr. Donodio, I will be glad to have a word with you. Officer Chavez"—he inclined his head to the standing uniform—"please escort Melisande across the hall where she can wait her turn in comfort. Dr. Donodio may wait in the hall, and you stay there with him in case he strays."

"Now see here . . ." Brian began, but there was a hand under his elbow and an irresistible though not painful pressure urging him to the door. Officer Chavez was not a man to be trifled with, and he was discovering that Sergeant Connolly could not be trifled with either.

12

THE AER LINGUS jet *St. Ciaran* winged serenely over the North Atlantic at thirty-five thousand feet. The tourist cabin was crowded with families on vacation, tense young adults coming to the United States in hope of finding work, and Americans returning home.

In the Premier Class cabin the Sullivans rode in solitary splendor, courtesy of Aer Lingus. There had been no tourist seats available when they called to explain their awful errand, but a sympathetic ticket agent had booked them anyway, even though Dualta Sullivan had explained that they didn't have the money.

"Don't you worry, Mr. Sullivan. I'll just put you down at the low fare and we'll find an empty corner to tuck you and Mrs. Sullivan in. It's a dreadful thing that's happened"—the story was front-page news all over Ireland—"and we're all sorry for your troubles."

Dualta had always wanted to fly. It was one of the many things he never had been able to afford on the wage he earned at Bord na Mona. With the children coming one after the other, it had been as much as he could manage to fill their bellies and keep shoes on their feet. Cutting the turf didn't pay enough for luxuries when there were seven little ones at home.

At his side, Grania wept softly into her handkerchief. They sat rigidly, their bodies not touching, a lifetime of public decorum holding them separate even now. When she spoke her voice was so low and dull he had to bend his ear to her lips.

"That New York policeman, Sergeant Connolly, he said we had to come and identify the . . ." She hesitated, unable to say the word *body*, as if by saying it she granted reality. "Could it possibly be, God forgive me for wishing this on someone else, that it's not our Maureen at all, but some other poor soul?"

"It's her all right." Misery made his voice harsh. "Didn't he say they had her passport and her warrant card? Don't be getting your hopes up. I told her nothing good could come out of her joining the Garda."

"It's got nothing to do with the Garda. She went to New York to find Monica. And where is Monica? Two of our children . . ." Her shoulders hunched and the deep sobs she fought to suppress came gushing.

The soft voice of the flight attendant broke through their wall of misery. "Come with me, Mrs. Sullivan. I'll get some cold water to wash your face, then you can have a nice cup of tea and lie down. Heaven knows there are enough empty seats that the two of you don't have to sit crowded together. And you, Mr. Sullivan, we have more than three hours before we land at Kennedy. Would you like a drink to help pass the time?"

"I'd not say no to a pint."

"I'll bring it right away. Then it will be time for lunch, and before you know it we'll be landing. Come on now, Mrs. Sullivan."

Dualta eyed her gratefully. Another woman was what Grania needed now. They were a grand bunch, these hostesses. It was a good job for a woman. Not like his Maureen. What sort of girl joined the Garda? He remembered when she

64

was little, always tearing around with a bunch of boys, her hair a mess, her knees always scarred. Grania begged him to allow her to wear trousers, even the nuns at school took him aside and suggested she be allowed to wear them, but he was adamant. No daughter of his would wear trousers. By the time she was fourteen he wished she was back playing with the boys. They were still coming around, but they had different games on their minds. He'd yelled and forbidden her to go out at night, and once, God help him, he'd slapped her across the mouth. The only time he'd ever raised his hand to a woman.

Then there was the time she'd finished her police training. He'd tried not to show it after all the fuss he'd made, but, by God, he was proud of her in her trim blue uniform when she was sworn in. She was the best looking of the bunch. Top of her class, too. His shoulders hunched a little more and his grip on his glass tightened. He'd never told her of his pride. Instead he'd continued to grouse and grumble to her face, even while he was boasting about her to his mates at the pub. And letting them think he had all sorts of inside information. Truth was Maureen never talked to him about her work. Everything he knew he got secondhand from Grania. That was how he found out she was in a special course to learn computers.

The voice of the captain came over the intercom. Dualta's mind grasped at the man's words. "We'll be landing at Kennedy Airport at three-fifteen New York time. Temperature there is eighty-two degrees and it's clear. A very nice day."

"A nice day," his mind echoed bitterly.

"Mr. Sullivan"—the hostess touched his shoulder—"I have a message for you from a Sergeant Connolly. He and a Mr. Donodio will be meeting your flight. Mr. and Mrs. Donodio have offered to put you and Mrs. Sullivan up for your stay."

"Thank you. What kind of name would Donodio be? Have you any idea?"

65

"I'd say Italian."

Dualta reflected in silence on the hostess's information. He had never known any Italians. Why would an unknown Italian family invite him and Grania to be their guests? But they're not Italians, he reflected, any more than Sergeant Connolly is an Irishman, in spite of his name. They're all Yanks, and everyone knows Yanks are crazy.

Soon his lunch came. He ate it without tasting, glad to see that Grania still slept in the chair opposite. He thought of waking her but the hostess stopped him. "The sleep will do her more good than the food. I'll call her with a cup of tea and a snack before we land."

He nodded assent. If truth were told, it wasn't just for Grania's sake he was glad she slept. Soon he found himself nodding. He snapped awake, feeling that to give in was somehow disloyal to Maureen, but nature overruled him. He fell fathoms deep into a black velvet refuge where Maureen was again a freckle-faced tomboy and Monica tagged after her elder sister like a wriggly puppy.

13

THE INTERNATIONAL ARRIVALS Building at JFK swarmed. It seemed to Brian that all of the continents had given a mighty flip and sent their surplus people spinning across the oceans, over the poles, around the horns, through the canals, over the tundras, bypassing grandmother's house, to land in the Big Apple.

"Please excuse." He hopped aside as a crocodile of Japanese businessmen, blue suited, white shirted, horn rimmed, camera bedecked, clove the crowds with single-minded, polite purpose.

In another corner lights and cameras were trained on a team of Taiwanese gymnasts who bounced like rubber through the air to land on their teammates' shoulders in a pyramid. Their sweating impresario was trying to explain in a thirty-second bite for the six o'clock news why this was the most extraordinary performance ever presented and why it was every American's patriotic duty to see them on their limited three-week engagement.

Brian was still smarting over Con's treatment of him the previous evening. To compound matters, he knew he had been wrong. He certainly had violated the spirit of his noninterference commitment to Deirdre, if not the letter.

When Con finally had called him in all he said was, "Dr. Donodio, I know you're interested and concerned, but have you stopped to consider that you may be placing Deirdre in serious danger? By now the murderer knows you found Maureen's body, and he may wonder what else you know and, by extension, what Deirdre knows. Please, just leave it to the professionals. I really would hate to be investigating Deirdre's murder as well as Maureen's."

Deirdre's voice interrupted. "They should be announcing the flight any minute now."

As if in response the loudspeaker clicked over their heads. "Aer Lingus flight from Shannon now arriving." Brian felt a tightening in his gut. What did a man say to strangers in these circumstances? He had felt that the least he could do was to offer hospitality in person, a shoulder to lean on. He shuddered in empathy. What if it had been Deirdre or Maria? He rose to his feet.

"Sit down," Deirdre's hand was on his arm, pulling him back to his seat. "It'll be some time yet. They have to clear customs and wait for their luggage. We might as well sit for a bit."

"She's right, sir."

Both Con and Deirdre had insisted on coming with him to meet the Sullivans. Brian had demurred, but Con's logic was flawless.

"It will be easier if there are three of us. Besides, I can park a police car in a no-parking zone. If you go alone you'll have to use the parking lot, then leave them when you go to fetch the car. Easier all the way round if you do it our way." The "our" was accompanied by a swift glance at Deirdre that she affected not to notice.

The truth of the matter was that he was a coward. A grade-A, homogenized, stone washed, prime cut, deluxe coward. Before bringing the Sullivans to the house, Con and Deirdre were taking them to the morgue to identify Maureen. Brian did not think he could bear it, watching them go into

68

the morgue, cherishing a forlorn hope that it was all a terrible mistake. Seeing them crumple as the truth hit home.

"I can't bear it," he murmured.

Deirdre hugged his arm. "Yes you can. Just think how much easier it will be for them to have someone who really cares with them. Someone their own age. Someone who has children. You can empathize more than Con and I ever could, even though my heart is near to bursting."

"She's right, sir."

"Is that all you know how to say?" Brian instantly regretted his waspish tone.

"No, but in this case I'm right. She's right."

"Yes, Dad. He's right. I'm right."

They looked at each other and started to laugh.

"What's so funny?"

"Nothing." Con was serious now. "But most cops learn to make jokes or they would go nuts." He glanced at his watch. "They should be coming out any minute. Let's go over to the gate."

The first few passengers were just straggling out. Con tapped Deirdre on the shoulder and pointed.

"See those two being shepherded by the Aer Lingus attendant? Either they're VIPs or our pigeons."

"I'll find out." Brian squared his shoulders resolutely and walked over.

"Excuse me," he tipped his hat and smiled, "am I addressing Mr. and Mrs. Sullivan?"

"You are. And who might you be?" Dualta's voice was flat. A man going through the motions.

"I'm Brian Donodio." He took a deep breath. Lord, he thought, let me find the right words. "I can't say 'welcome to New York,' as I'd like to. All I can say is my wife Maire and I are sorrier than we can say. We hope you will accept our home as yours while you are here."

The hostess smiled. "Then I'll leave you in Mr. Donodio's hands."

"This way." He scooped up their one suitcase and

69

cupped Grania's elbow with his free hand. "My daughter Deirdre and Sergeant Connolly are waiting." He steered them through the crowded lobby, past couples embracing in joyous reunion, past bored professional drivers holding placards aloft, past harassed tour guides mustering their queues of tourists like nervous collies.

"Con went to get the car. He'll meet us outside." Deirdre turned to Grania, who was bewildered by the noise and confusion. "I knew Maureen and I liked her so much. She and I spent several very happy times together. I can't begin to tell you how sorry I am."

"You're in the police like our Maureen?"

"Not the regular police like she was." Deirdre did not elaborate as she moved them to the door. "Con, whom you'll meet in a moment, is with the New York City police."

The automatic door slid open. Con was parked outside, ignoring the hoots of cabs and private cars waiting to disgorge and pick up. A uniformed police officer and an airport security guard were bearing down on him from opposite sides. The uniform glanced at the plate and waved the airport man back.

When they reached the car the uniformed officer relieved Brian of the suitcase. Brian glanced at his name tag. "O'Hagan."

"Thank you, Officer O'Hagan."

"You're welcome, sir. And I'm sorry for your trouble, Mr. and Mrs. Sullivan. Maureen was one of our own, and we'll get the bastard."

Con put the car in gear and maneuvered through the airport traffic. "I'm going to go straight downtown. I know it's hard, but the best thing is for you to identify Maureen straightaway, then I'll take you out to Woodside."

Grania's control broke. Tears welled up and streamed down her face as her body shook with the sobs she tried vainly to repress. From her mouth came a suppressed mewing like a kitten in pain.

"Mrs. Sullivan can wait outside."

70

"Man, have you no heart at all?" Dualta's voice cracked.

Grania shrugged away from Deirdre's arm and a long shudder shook her body. She reached somewhere inside to the reserve of strength held by generations of Irish mothers who had seen their children drown, starve, die of wasting sickness, emigrate for life, sold into slavery in Barbados, die in foreign armies, in civil war, in resistance to the foreign invader; this heritage of horror steeled her now.

"No." Her voice had steadied. "I'll see my child, kiss her forehead, and bid her farewell. It's my right, and no one shall take it from me."

"And no one shall, Mrs. Sullivan," said Brian. Sensing that the moment was right and that it would ease her pain, he asked, "Would you tell us something about her?"

"Of all the seven, she was the one with a way about her. When she came into the room people smiled, the talk got lighter. She drew out the best in people, made them seem smarter and funnier than they were. Ah, she was a great girl. Her father was not happy that she joined the Garda, but it was what she wanted, and what she wanted was what she usually got."

"And see where it got her," growled Dualta.

"Then she was on police business?" Deirdre let the question float on the air.

"Nothing of the sort. It's just a bee he has in his bonnet. Her being here has nothing to do with police work. She would have been here even if she worked behind a counter in a draper's shop."

"Why did she come?"

The rush hour traffic was heavy on the Van Wyck Expressway. There was plenty of time to talk before they reached the tunnel.

"Our Monica, she's the next sister to Maureen, but two of the boys came between, finished her schooling. She went to university and trained as a teacher, but there was no job at all for her in Ireland when she finished. The unemployment is

71

terrible. So Monica and a couple of her friends set their hearts on coming to the States."

"Were they coming on vacation or as immigrants?"

"They had great plans, the three of them. I was worried about the immigration, but Monica kept telling me not to worry, they had that all fixed."

Deirdre thought of the computer entry listing Monica Sullivan as a legal immigrant and of the curious lack of paperwork to back the entry. She opened her mouth to question further, then closed it again; this was no time to add a further burden to the Sullivans' backs.

"At first we got letters, then they stopped coming, and when we wrote, the letters came back from the American post office marked 'unknown.' We tried calling, but the number we had was disconnected. Maureen told us not to get the police mixed up in it in case Monica was mixed up in something illegal, she'd rather come over herself and have a look around . . ." Her voice trailed off as she fumbled inside her bag and brought out her rosary, clutching at the beads as though courage would flow from them for the ordeal ahead.

Too soon they emerged from the Midtown Tunnel and turned south to the grim building near the East River that marked the end of so many dreams. Dualta and Grania moved slowly, their dread mirrored in dragging feet. In Brian's hypersensitive state he seemed to sense an apartness about them, a dignity and consequence not normally theirs. A line of Oscar Wilde's floated into his head: "Where there is sorrow, there is holy ground. . . ." His eyes skittered around the small viewing room and came to rest on the wide, low, curtained window. Grania's arm was shaking in his hand, the rhythms of grief and fear in horrid counterpoint to her shuddering breath. Dualta held himself rigidly erect, his hat over his heart, feet spread wide as if to draw strength from the solid floor beneath. He heard Deirdre catch her breath in a half sob.

"Sit here, Mrs. Sullivan." Brian's hand urged her to a waiting chair.

The curtain parted. Maureen lay on the stretcher with a sheet drawn up so only her face showed. Someone's kindly hand had combed her hair and made sure it covered the ravages of the pathologist's knife. Grania struggled to her feet.

"I'm going to her."

Con nodded. "Come with me."

When the Sullivans left the room, the curtain closed. Brian and Deirdre looked at each other. "Why did she have to go back there, Dad?"

He was irrationally angry. "How the hell should I know? To touch, to feel, to say good-bye. The only one who could answer that is Grania. How long will they be staying?"

"Only till tomorrow. The coroner's releasing the body and they're taking her home tomorrow night. Con made all the arrangements."

14

SIX O'CLOCK ON a bright summer morning is perfection in New Rumple, New York. Thaddeus Putankowski cycled along the outskirts of the town delivering his carefully folded papers to the widely spaced houses. Most of the houses had forgotten their origins as working farms. Now they gleamed in a perfection of white paint, interiors glowing with the instant ambience purveyed by Laura Ashley and Ralph Lauren. Thad himself lived in Spruce Island west of the town, on a real farm where the principal crop was the handsome brown onion that added so much flavor to people's lives.

He picked his way carefully down the flagstone path at Dr. Gebhardt's and whistled to Walesa, his dog of indeterminate provenance. Walesa was nowhere to be seen.

From his apartment window the man watched the dog. First it sniffed and circled, then started to dig frantically at the brighter green rectangle. Even from this distance he could see the animal's fur standing in a ridge down its spine. Then it snapped something up in its mouth and raced off toward the road.

Time to be moving on. Packing didn't take long. A few clothes, his gun, and the flat, black case that held the software. He always had been meticulous about keeping the place clean and polished, so a few minutes with spray cleaner and a soft cloth around the light switches and the bathroom should take care of scattered prints. He even remembered to wipe the underside of the toilet seat.

Shortly thereafter a beige Honda passed Thad, who was looking in horror at the trophy presented him by Walesa. He didn't glance at the car.

Walesa's find lay at Thad's feet. At first glance it looked like a brown twig with something red on the end, then it snapped into focus. It was a human finger with a red-polished nail still attached.

15

IT HAD BEEN a bad two days. Brian and Deirdre let themselves into the house after seeing the Sullivans off to Ireland.

"I'll never forget your kindness . . ." Grania's conventional words had slipped away in a film of tears.

"And next time you come to Ireland you must stay with us," Dualta had added.

"You'll see me coming up the garden path one of these days." They knew it was a lie.

There were a couple of hours of daylight left. Brian felt the need to get his hands in the earth, to wash away death in clean soil. He'd been meaning to attack the perennial border, to get everything perfect for Maire's show tomorrow. The arabis needed thinning. The Siberian iris were starting to overwhelm the coreopsis. He tried to clear his mind and let his hands think, let them draw up the earth's healing. And if I feel battered and spiritually sick, he thought, how must the Sullivans feel? He had watched Grania storing up the pain, making it part of herself. Hiding it here and there on her person, shoved down into the corners of her mind, swelling her heart to bursting. She would move through her grief with quiet dignity, her tongue quick with ready excuses for Dualta.

He was sure that Dualta, once the first shock of grief had passed, would take a pride that might almost be called relish in his role. Now his drinking buddies would show new respect and tell his story in hushed tones to strangers at the pub, and he would thrive on it . . .

Brian clipped savagely. God forgive me, maybe I'm being too hard on the poor fellow. Maybe it's just that I see in him what I myself could become in a similar position. At the thought a wave of depression washed over him and he drew his thoughts away.

All around him was frantic activity. The committee from St. Enda's was setting up the refreshment tent. A florist delivered masses of cut flowers for the house. Brian's suggestion that they come from his garden had been vetoed by a superior whippersnapper in tight jeans and hexagonal glasses.

What now? A van proclaiming "GODWOT'S, WHERE A GARDEN IS A LOVESOME THING" skittered up to the curb. The men jumped out and started to unload. By God, they were unloading plaster ducks, gnomes, and mushrooms. No way. He'd willingly die for Maire, but he would not put up with those atrocities on his lawn. He charged into action.

"What's going on?"

The driver, a large man with a red face, pushed his button-adorned cap back on his head and pulled a sheaf of crumpled invoices from his pants pocket.

"Donodio?"

"That's right."

"Sign." He shoved the papers in Brian's face.

"No. I didn't order this stuff."

"You're Donodio?"

"I said I was."

"Then I got your order, and I don't got all day."

All of the emotions of the last four days suddenly boiled up inside him. "Why, you . . ." he spluttered. A red mist grew in front of his eyes and he drew back his fist to smash the thick red face in front of him.

His arm was caught efficiently by Con, who had been sitting with Deirdre in the arbor.

"Come over here and sit down, sir," he murmured as he applied gentle pressure. "Deirdre, deal with this fellow. I guess your dad doesn't like ducks."

Brian found himself in the arbor. As suddenly as it had boiled up, his rage receded, leaving him drained and shaking.

16

SUNDAY WAS A triumph of artifice. By ten o'clock the first of the chartered buses arrived, loaded with two garden clubs from New Haven. Hot on their heels came TV crews from PBS and "Eyewitness News." *The New York Times* sent a charming gray-haired woman who spent two minutes in the house and two hours in the garden. The grandchildren's room boasted golden-haired boy and girl twins from the Modish Moppet Talent Agency. The boy wore a sailor suit, the girl was pure Tenniel in a pale blue *Alice in Wonderland* dress and ribbon. Refreshments did a brisk business, as did St. Enda's parking lot and the country craft booth manned by the ladies of the Altar and Rosary Society.

Brian patrolled the garden, on the qui vive for fellow gardeners not above sneaking a cutting or two. Enough of them can ruin a rare plant in short order. He caught two red-handed and skewered several suspects with his eye.

At about two o'clock, when the crowd was thickest, a van drew up driven by Barney Finucane. Six people got out. Considering the terms on which they'd parted, Brian wanted to hide in his study. But there was no escape, the man had spotted him.

Thursday might never have happened. There was a broad smile on Finucane's face and his hand was outstretched.

"Dr. Donodio, we thought we'd come and see what you're up to out in Queens, give St. Enda's a boost." He gestured at the group crowding behind him. "I'm sure you know most of these good people."

"These good people" shifted from one foot to the other, looking embarrassed. Brian didn't blame them. It was a hateful way to describe anyone. There was the dancing teacher, grinning toothily, whose name turned out to be Bridget Brannigan. Three were from his class—two were the old pensioners who enjoyed napping, the other was Patrick Garrity, the fellow who knew more Irish history than he did.

But who was the girl? Her face was familiar. By God, it was Melisande. A changed Melisande. No longer was her hair dyed three different colors, it was shaven. Gone was the safety pin in her ear; in its place was a demure gold stud. Gone were the rag-bag layers of thrift store garments. From neck to toe she was sleekly attired in black. He looked again and felt his ears get red. That garment she had on top, was that what they called a bustier? Women!

"*Cead mille failte,* a hundred thousand welcomes," he said heartily, hoping against hope that his pronunciation wasn't too dreadful. "Come and let me give you the grand tour."

Garrity turned slowly to take in the vista. "My God, what a picture."

"It's been my hobby for years, and I'm pleased at the result."

"Man, you should be. My sister at home is a great gardener, and I know how much work it is."

They toured the grounds rapidly. As they passed the refreshment tent Brian said, "Nothing in there but soda, tea, and cranberry juice. Maybe you'd fancy a real drink with me in my study after you've seen the house. Just wait a minute while I have a word with one of the men from St. Enda's. We have to watch that no one takes cuttings from the plants."

80

Inside, Maire and Deirdre were taking the tours in turn, shepherding visitors around in groups of ten. On display were the living and dining rooms, the kitchen, the grandchildren's room, and Brian and Maire's bedroom transformed into a ruffled retreat. The bathrooms remained true to their function.

Barney advanced on Deirdre with a broad smile. "I hoped I would see you today." He nodded at Maire. "Is this charming lady your mother?"

"And my wife," Brian interposed firmly before he performed the introductions. "Now, anyone who wishes can tour the house with Maire and Deirdre, or you are welcome to a drink in my study. It's off limits for the tour."

Barney and Patrick Garrity opted for the drink. Melisande, the dancing teacher, and the three old people went off to look at the house. Brian felt uncomfortable. He could feel a tension, as though they wanted something but didn't know where to begin. Barney he could understand, but Patrick? He busied himself with drinks, then sat behind the desk.

"Slainte," he lifted his glass.

"Slainte," they echoed dutifully.

The silence dragged out. Maureen Sullivan's murder trembled at the lip of his mind, but he had promised Con and Deirdre last night that he was through playing cop, and he meant to keep his word. That is . . .

Barney cleared his throat. "It's about this terrible thing that happened."

"Yes?"

"I was up in Boston," Patrick chimed in. "I read about it in the papers, but I never realized that it was the Maureen I knew, God rest her, until Barney told me where she came from. I know the whole family. Dualta and Grania come from Ballyglenfoyle, you see."

Well, Brian thought, it's being thrust upon me. If I call Deirdre in I'll blow her cover.

"Where are you from, Patrick?"

81

"A little town on the west coast called Portnoo; you won't have heard of it. It's not far from Ballyglenfoyle."

"Do you know Monica?"

"Sure I know Monica. Real little imp. Then, suddenly, she was sixteen and she changed. Old Dualta had to use the broom to sweep the boys off the doorstep. Why? What's she up to?"

"No one seems to know. She came here to find work and she's disappeared. Maureen came over to try and find her. Here, let me freshen your drinks."

Brian shrugged and picked up the whiskey bottle.

"She'll turn up sooner or later. There are no flies on Sergeant Connolly." He topped up the glasses. "If she doesn't report when she's supposed to as a registered alien, the INS will be after her."

The air conditioner was going in the study window but the sweat stood out on both Finucane's and Garrity's foreheads.

AFTER THE OPEN house Con and Deirdre went out for the first time. Con had planned mightily to make it perfect. Too perfect, in Deirdre's opinion. A relentlessly nouvelle cuisine dinner she was sure cost more than he could afford. "Mostly Mozart" at Lincoln Center followed by a drive out to Rockaway for drinks on the dock of Pier 92, a surprising restaurant with its entrance hidden behind a McDonald's. The owner, an old friend of Con's, was not there tonight.

He was looking out across Jamaica Bay. The next move would be to reach for her hand, gaze compellingly into her baby blues, and say (throatily), "Your place or mine?" She did hope she was wrong. No, he was turning.

"Dammit, Deirdre, can't you persuade your old man to stay out of police business? Last night he swore he was through with playing detective, then he got right into it again today."

Unreasonably, she was piqued. Her answer was tart. "How do you persuade the cat to stay out of the catnip? At least he told us everything this time."

"Well, it's dangerous. I told him that already. Dangerous for you as well as for him."

Deirdre rummaged in her bag and came up with a notebook. Turning to a fresh page she said, "Let's make a list; with all the excitement today we haven't had a chance to discuss the case."

"Okay."

"First. Have you come up with the tenant of record on the Twenty-second Street apartment?"

"For all the good it does us, yes. The guy has a sense of humor. Would you believe Oscar Wilde?"

"What about the lease?"

"No lease. Month-to-month tenancy. And he pays with postal money orders with a typed-in signature. What about the computer record on Monica?"

"That's all in order; it shows a green card issued last September, and to the two friends Grania told us about. We're still waiting to hear from Dublin about the paperwork. It's weird, so far they haven't come up with any, nor has the Irish government. I wish they'd get themselves in gear. It's been six days since Dad found Maureen's body."

"Bureaucrats!" In Con's mouth the word was an epithet. "We've put a missing persons out on Monica. Patrick Garrity has an alibi for Tuesday night. Boston confirmed it, but they tell me not to put too much faith in it. The guys he claims to be with would alibi the Son of Sam if it suited them."

"Dandy. Anything on the search of the flat?"

"Nothing but Maureen's stuff and cat traces. A lot of smudges, no useful prints. The lab came up with something cosmetic spilled on that pillow under Maureen's head. Some type of perfume, but they're having trouble with the ingredients. Probably doesn't mean anything."

"Have you asked Dad about it?" Deirdre explained about her father's educated nose.

"Now that sounds really crazy. But everything about your family's crazy. Okay, I'll have him down to the station to sniff."

"Any trace of Sean Morrissey, if that's his real name? You know, I nearly dropped my teeth when I walked into the

84

Four Green Fields on Thursday and saw Dad sitting at the bar. We've had our eye on that place for months."

"Nothing so far. We have a good description, thanks to your dad—I'll say that for him—and we're keeping the bar under surveillance. If Morrissey hasn't been scared off, we may grab him. It was smart of your dad to get his prints on the glass."

A nippy little breeze whipped in from the bay. Deirdre shivered and Con took advantage of the shiver to shift to her side of the table and drape a solicitous arm across her bare shoulders.

"You must be freezing in that light dress. Would you like my jacket?"

"And expose your arsenal to the malefactors of Rockaway? No thanks." She decided to be a shameless hussy. "Your arm feels cozy, though."

The cozy arm cozied her in a little closer. "I always follow my mother's advice."

"And that is?"

"Remember, son, a good woman appreciates a cozy arm on a cold night."

Surely it was just accident that placed her ear so close to his lips. "Your ear is cold, too. May I warm it a little?"

"Just a little."

And a little, and a little, and a little.

And there was a little cough behind them. "Excuse me, folks. I just thought you should know that we're getting ready to close soon."

Not knowing whether she was glad or sorry, but certain that she was embarrassed, Deirdre glanced at her watch. "It's after midnight and we have a full day coming up."

Con threw the waiter a dirty look and was rewarded by a complacent smirk. "Let's go."

They were silent as they drove across the bridge, through Broad Channel and the Jamaica Bay Wildlife Preserve. When Crossbay turned into Woodhaven Boulevard, Deirdre spoke. "To change the subject, I want to run an idea for you. We can't check it until we have confirmation of lack of paperwork from Dublin, but here goes. I think we have a computer crime and the murder was committed to keep it covered up. Suppose someone, either here or in Ireland, got into the INS data bank and was issuing phony green cards. Suppose people pay to have their names entered in the computer. Then, when they've been in the U.S. for a few months, they report a lost card to the INS. They fill out a jillian forms in triplicate, the machine grinds into action, and a few weeks later, presto!

"Mrs. Sullivan told us Maureen was a hacker for the Garda. Suppose Maureen caught on to what was happening. I'm sure the Irish authorities have some way to cross-check with the INS."

"Why wouldn't she report it on the Irish end?" A cab came barreling out of Myrtle Avenue to hang an illegal left as Con's brakes screeched and the smell of burned rubber came floating through the window. "Damn cabbies. Why is there never a cop around when you need one?"

"Because the cops are too busy sweet-talking ladies on docks in Rockaway. But to get to your first question, Monica is her sister, and cops don't want their families mixed up with the fuzz any more than anyone else. Suppose Maureen voiced her fears to the fellow who loaned her the Twenty-second Street apartment. We already know there's something funny going on there."

Con reached out and grabbed her hand. "You have a lot of 'supposes' there, but they make sense. What do you think we should do?"

Her hand felt so good in his. "We have to wait for the idiots in Dublin. I wish we had enough to get a warrant to search the center and get one of our own hackers busy on that terminal on Finucane's desk."

"So do I, but we have to wait for Dublin."

Calvary Cemetery was looming up on the left with its floodlit cross stark against the night. Deirdre shuddered. Con squeezed her hand tighter.

"Ah, it's not so bad, acushla. So far it's been a pretty good life." He stole a hopeful, sideways glance. "And I have a feeling it's going to get a lot better."

"Con, I have a key to the Irish center. Why do we have to wait for Dublin? We can go now and just take a little look around."

"But we don't have a warrant."

"Do we need one? I work there. I need to powder my nose."

"But . . ."

"But what? We're not breaking and entering. I have a key and I have the right to be there. Let's go."

"It's iffy, but okay, you're on." Traffic was slowing down ahead, a red river of tail lights stretching out to the Queensborough Bridge. He put the flasher on the roof and touched the siren. "Let's go in style."

18

.T THE IRISH center the printer popped out the last sheet and :ame to a halt.

"That's it, then." The man grabbed the neatly stacked pile and put it in his briefcase. "You're sure there are no other printouts of anything?"

Barney Finucane was shifting uneasily in his chair and sweating. "That's it, I swear." He busied himself erasing the disks.

"You could have managed better, you know." The man's voice was dispassionate. "Killing Monica was unnecessary."

"What the hell was I supposed to do? She said she'd thought things over and decided she, and these are her exact words, didn't 'want to be mixed up with a bunch of terrorists.'"

"She had her green card. There was no danger she'd go to the American authorities. Fear of being deported would have kept her mouth shut. And now you tell me they've found the body."

"But they can't tie it to me," Barney protested. "I rented that place under a false name and cleared everything out when I left."

"What name did you rent under?"

"Charles S. Parnell." There was a touch of "see what a clever boy I am" in his tone.

"Jaysus!" The man's head shook with disgust. "They picked a real winner in you. And you had the place on Twenty-second Street under the name of Oscar Wilde! Even the Yanks aren't so dumb they can't make that connection. And you drink, and sniff coke. You'd split like a paper bag in a cloudburst if the cops picked you up."

Barney's eyes were darting from right to left. "It wasn't me that stabbed Maureen."

"You might as well have. You were there and you're going to take the credit."

"What do you mean, take the credit?" A blob of spittle appeared on the corner of his mouth.

The man made an impatient gesture. "Just write on a piece of paper 'I'm sorry about Maureen, Monica, and Donodio. I don't know why I did it,' and sign your name. Stop blubbering like a five year old. You know we take care of our own." He reached inside his briefcase and pulled out an envelope. "Here you are, your new passport is in the name of Brian Borhu, since you are so fond of the Irish names, and the ticket is for Brazil via Toronto. You'll go straight to JFK from here and catch the early flight to Canada. Now write."

"What about money?"

"There's plenty here." He fanned a large stack of greenbacks.

Barney finished writing. "Now what?"

"Now we have to get rid of Donodio. I know he suspects something. He was as fidgety as a cat in heat at that damn open house of his, and we have no way of knowing what Maureen may have told that daughter of his who's always nosing around." His eyes met the eyes of the watcher in the corner and a nod of agreement passed between them. "Here's what I want you to do. . . ."

19

Light was streaming from a second-floor window when Con and Deirdre drove silently up to the center.

"Uh-oh, looks like we've got company." Con turned to Deirdre. "You still want to go in?"

"Why not?"

He slid his gun out of the holster as she reached inside her bag for hers. "Better let me go first."

"And why should I?" She slipped off her high-heeled sandals and moved barefoot across the pavement.

"You can't go in there barefoot," he protested in a furious whisper.

"Fat lot of good I'd be in a scuffle with high heels."

By now they were standing on either side of the door. Deirdre reached out a cautious hand and pushed. To their surprise, the door moved soundlessly inward.

"Side door," Deirdre mouthed, pointing to the darkened areaway leading to the basement.

Con nodded and was turning when a taxi pulled up and Brian emerged. There was a sudden rush of feet as two figures raced from under the stairs, knocking Deirdre and Con to the sidewalk. The pair leaped into a waiting car and sped off. By the time they got up, all they saw was disappearing tail lights.

All three spoke at once. "What the hell . . . ?"

Deirdre was first to recover. She scooped up her gun and surveyed her dress ruefully. There was a long rip up the side and indelible marks of Manhattan sidewalk all over her rear. "You okay, Con?"

"Nothing hurt but my dignity. Well, nothing we can do now about those two, they got clean away." He turned to Brian, who was still goggling. "What brings you here?"

"You won't believe this, but I had a call from Finucane. He said there was something urgent he had to discuss and it couldn't wait till morning. I left a message for you at the station and they said they'd get in touch with you."

As if in answer, the beeper on Con's belt stuttered to life.

"Did you get a look at those two?"

"They were wearing ski masks."

"Well, let's go in."

Within, all was silent, the stairs lit by a vagrant gleam from Finucane's second-floor office. Guns out, Con and Deirdre went first and took their positions on either side of the office door. Not a sound, not a rustle, but Brian's head snapped up as he sniffed. Cigarettes, gunpowder, dust, and, yes, there it was. Spicy, tangy—the same smell that had lingered around Maureen's body.

"Police officers, freeze!" Con yelled as he jumped through the door, his gun held two handed, legs apart.

But there was no one living to obey his order. Finucane slumped forward in his chair with his right hand resting on the desk, loosely curled around a Ruger Bearcat .22. Behind his right ear was a hole peppered around the edge with powder burns. Con's hands automatically went into his pockets as he studied the scene and Deirdre's folded across her chest.

"Come in, Dad," she called, "but don't touch anything. Keep your hands in your pockets."

91

Brian felt caught inside a Saturday night movie. This was not real.

"What does it say?" Deirdre pointed with her chin to the note on the desk.

" 'I'm sorry about Maureen, Monica, and Donodio, I don't know why I did it.' "

Con whistled. "I think you're a very lucky man. If Deirdre hadn't talked me into coming here for a look around you'd have walked right into it. As it is they saw our car, assumed it was you, then wasted Finucane so he could take the rap for all three murders. Then, when they saw who was getting out of the car, they made a run for it. They should have grabbed the note, but fortunately for us, they made a mistake."

"And we might have bought it," added Deirdre, "if they'd had time to set it up convincingly. The third murder, then an attack of remorse. And I'm sure that whoever they are, they're happy to get rid of Barney. A user, an alcoholic, and a womanizer, not much of an asset. Well, my cover's blown."

"I'd better get down to the car and call this in." Con saw that Brian was trembling. "Are you all right? Here, why don't you and Deirdre wait downstairs in the lounge."

Brian visibly brought himself under control. "I'm a bit shaken. Who wouldn't be? But don't you notice the smell?"

"What smell?"

"The same smell that was in that unspeakable apartment on Twenty-second Street. Whoever shot Finucane either is the same person who knifed Maureen or, at least, was there during the murder."

20

"They're probably in Saudi Arabia or Brazil," Brian fussed at Deirdre.

"Possibly," she agreed calmly. "Or they may be right here in the U.S., going about their business. We don't have a single fact to hang on them, not even names."

Smith came marching proudly out of the bushes to lay a vole in tribute at Brian's feet. She jumped up on his lap to gain her due meed of praise.

"Why can't you talk, Smith?"

"She has, in a way. The lab matched her hair to hairs found in Finucane's office. It's not conclusive because we've all had contact with the cat, but it's another thread to link the crimes together."

Deirdre had come straight to the house after finishing at the center and she was nearly dropping on her feet after the night's events. She was meeting Con so they could go over the latest discoveries. Brian had slept most of the day away. He was rested and bubbling with curiosity.

A car slowed down at the corner and turned into the drive.

"That's Con, now. Dad, it's okay for you to listen, but please, you have to stay out of this."

Con came around the corner of the house. His eyes were red rimmed and he needed a shave.

"You look like something Smith would refuse to drag in," was Deirdre's greeting.

"More to the point, how about a beer?" asked Brian.

"I'd fall flat on my face."

"Iced tea?"

"Great." Con pulled a sheaf of papers from his briefcase. "We've heard from Dublin."

"The plot thickens, Watson." Deirdre fought back a yawn. "What have we heard?"

"The hackers on both sides of the water are having a field day. Someone has definitely been in the data banks and they're going to have to authenticate every green card issued for the last two years."

"But that will take months," Deirdre objected.

"Well, that's their problem. And, listen to this, they have to check all the countries, not just Ireland. They're afraid whoever did this may have been selling cards internationally."

Brian listened avidly, the iced tea forgotten.

"What about Patrick Garrity?"

"He's legal, with paperwork to back it up, but . . ."

Brian could contain himself no longer. "But *what?*"

Con glanced at Deirdre. "Tell him," she said resignedly. "If you don't he won't give us a moment's peace. I'll go get your iced tea. Wait till I get back."

"So tell me, what else have you smelled?"

"Well, all I can tell you is negative. Garrity had an after-shave I couldn't place, but that wasn't it. I know I've smelled that scent somewhere else, though. It'll come to me."

Just as Deirdre returned with the iced tea, Con's beeper interrupted with its peremptory stutter. "Oh, hell, what is it now?" He gestured to the cordless phone on the table. "May I?"

"Go ahead."

"Connolly here."

The conversation on Con's side was mostly grunts as he scribbled furiously on the piece of paper Deirdre had shoved under his pen. "Right," he concluded.

"It's coming together," he said as he hung up the phone. "Would you two like to take a ride upstate? I'll talk as we go along. Those Ulster County Republicans up in New Rumple have a victim who may be Monica."

"Jesus, Mary, and Joseph," said Brian, crossing himself. "Those poor people. This will finish Grania and Dualta."

They did not speak much as they rolled north on the Henry Hudson. Deirdre drove with Con snoring gently in the back seat. It was against regulations for her to drive an NYPD unmarked car, but who was to know? In the passenger seat Brian fidgeted impatiently.

"What was Con about to tell us when his beeper went off?"

Deirdre braked for the toll gate on the Tappan Zee Bridge. She clucked her tongue impatiently. "I'd rather he told you himself, and don't you go waking him up."

The green toll light flashed its "Thank you" and the car sped forward on the long, graceful bridge over the Hudson. To the right and left were the vistas beloved of generations of artists.

"Listen, Dad," Deirdre continued, "we have to wait for evidence that will stand up before a grand jury. God willing, we'll get that with a lot of routine digging. Your nose is valuable as an indication. If the lab can find something in Barney's office with that perfume on it, they can tie it to the same perfume found on the pillow under Maureen's head in Chelsea. That's evidence. Your smeller is only a lead."

Something else was on Brian's mind. "What gives between you and Con?"

Deirdre speeded up to pass a well-preserved 1956 Ford proceeding at a stately thirty-five miles per hour in the right lane. The driver, who probably had been middle aged when the car was new, shook his fist at her.

Out of deference to Brian's sensibilities, she confined

herself to muttering, "Idiot! What's between Con and me? Nothing, so far. I think I'm going to marry him, but he doesn't realize it yet."

"Wha-a-?"

"Calm down. It's bad for your blood pressure."

"But——"

"I'll observe the decencies. Con's a very conventional young man, and a very nice one. He'll get all upset if he doesn't have the fun of pursuit and conquest."

"Does your mother know anything about this?"

"We haven't discussed it, but I'm sure she'll understand. There are no flies on Mom."

The subject under discussion shifted in the backseat and whuffled gently. "Let's keep quiet now, he needs his sleep."

The long summer twilight had given way to dark when Deirdre turned in to the parking area by the remodeled Victorian Gothic railroad station that served the law and order needs of the citizens of New Rumple. They rousted Con, who stood, stretching hugely, trying to clear his head with deep lungsful of the clear Catskill air.

Behind a desk a uniformed officer looked up when they entered. His eyes flickered over Con's unshaven face and dismissed him. He looked at Brian. "May I help you?"

Con stepped forward and flipped open his wallet with the gold detective shield. "Sergeant Connolly, NYPD, Agent Donodio of the INS"—he nodded at Brian—"and this is Dr. Brian Donodio. We understand you may have the body of Monica Sullivan."

The officer came around the desk and shook hands. "Jim Svandalik." He called in the direction of a half-open door. "Chief, the officers from the city are here."

The chief was a small, neat, dark man with mean, squidgy eyes and a tight mouth. His uniform was sharply creased, his gun belt and shoes shone with hours of wifely polishing. His eyes passed over Con and he went to Brian with an outstretched hand. "Sergeant Connolly, welcome to New Rumple. I'm Chief Tierney."

Brian shook the outstretched hand. "Sorry, Chief, Sergeant Connolly is the handsome fellow here on my right. I'm Dr. Donodio, and this is Agent Donodio of the INS."

"I see," said Tierney sourly. He looked Con up and down, eyes marking the rumpled shirt and askew tie and dwelling overlong on chin stubble. He didn't even bother to acknowledge Deirdre. In his world, policing was men's business.

Con flashed his badge. "I'm short on sleep and time right now, Chief. Been up all night. May we see what you have?"

When they were seated in the inner office Tierney handed a set of papers over to Brian.

"Coroner's report, Dr. Donodio." Brian didn't disabuse him. He flicked over the pages with every evidence of intelligent interest, making appropriate grunts and "hmm's." When finished he handed the report to the fuming Con. Con read swiftly, then passed the report to Deirdre.

"What makes you think this poor soul was Monica Sullivan?"

"This, found buried with her." Tierney reached inside his desk and pulled out several paper evidence bags. "Purse, wallet with money and ID, including a green card and driver's license, tissues, cosmetics, keys, and several letters from Ireland.

"She was strangled, the hyoid bone was fractured . . ." He broke off to gaze in amazement at Brian.

He had eased open the evidence bags and, without touching or disturbing the contents, was sniffing each in turn. He shook his head. "Nothing. Too much to hope for after all this time."

Chief Tierney waited for an explanation. None was forthcoming.

"Interesting." Con turned to Deirdre. "Stabbing, shooting, and now strangulation. We have three different MO's."

"I hope to God we don't have three different killers," she answered. "Chief, we have a real mess here. At least four jurisdictions, an international computer crime that centers on the INS, with one of the victims a member of the Garda Siochana. It's a bureaucratic nightmare."

"What else do you have?" asked Con. "Any suspects? Anyone new in the area? Anyone moved out in a hurry? Above all, anyone with Irish connections?"

Chief Tierney leaned back in his chair and fastidiously raised his trousers to maintain their crease, displaying a neatly black-socked leg in the process. He flicked an imaginary speck off his shoulder and gazed complacently at them.

"No, to all your questions. As I see it, this has nothing to do with New Rumple."

"But . . ."

He raised his hand. "Oh, certainly the victim's body was found in my jurisdiction, but I'm sure that was accidental. Her grave was on the very outskirts of town where the houses are far apart. This has all the earmarks of a city crime; we were just unfortunate in having someone pick New Rumple to dispose of the body. Things like this just don't happen up here. We're not that kind of community." He ended with a complacent smirk.

Con forebore to comment on this incredible statement. "Well, may we have a copy of your videotape of the corpse and purse in situ?"

"Sure, for all the good it will do you. Now, is there anything else?"

Deirdre leaned forward. "Chief Tierney, I am an investigative agent in the Border Patrol Sector of the INS that has jurisdiction in this area. I would like a list of all the homeowners and tenants anywhere near the area in which Monica Sullivan's body was found. We have reason to believe that her murder is part of an ongoing case of large-scale illegal entry into the United States."

Tierney glowered and looked at Brian. "Are the two of you related?"

"My daughter."

"And you're an ME and on the same case she is?"

"Police work is a family tradition," said Brian obliquely.

"I know you're a busy man, Chief." Con leaned back and spread his legs in proper good-old-boy style, nudging Deirdre aside. "But you know how it is. Routine. You must have questioned the people around the area. Could we just have a look at the names?" He held up his hand when Tierney opened his mouth. "Most likely you're right. Why, I can tell just by looking at this lovely, peaceful place that no real citizen of New Rumple could be mixed up in something as sordid as this. But I have reports to write, and so does Agent Donodio." He paused expectantly.

Deirdre opened her mouth. Con kicked her ankle. Brian leaped in.

"Chief Tierney, man to man, and this is men's business (Deirdre was turning purple), could we just have a look at the statements from possible witnesses? You know, this is a big case. I can see the headline in *The New York Times:* CHIEF TIERNEY'S LEAD SOLVES CASE. That wouldn't hurt when you come up for reappointment, would it? It certainly would help if you ever think of running for elective office."

It was rather like blowing up a balloon, Brian thought. The man's head was getting bigger by the minute.

"Svandarlik," he yelled, "get off your ass and bring in the full file on Monica Sullivan."

"Sure thing, Chief," yelled Svandarlik, who appeared at the office door with the papers at the ready.

The three huddled together over the list. Suddenly Brian stiffened to attention and pointed.

"Charles S. Parnell. What do you know about him?"

Tierney waved a careless dismissal. "Why, nothing. As you can see, he was not at home. I'm sure he won't know anything about this. They have a very nice class of tenant in that house."

Deirdre brought out a picture of Barney. "Is this Parnell?"

"Never met Parnell," said Tierney impatiently. "But he does look familiar. I'm sure I've seen him around town. Why?"

"He's dead, Chief," answered Con. "Shot in the head last night with a Ruger Bearcat. He's the reason I haven't had time to shave."

On the return journey Brian asked Con, "Now, will you please tell me what you were going to say about Garrity when your beeper went off."

"He's missing."

21

THE SULLIVANS HAD come and gone, taking their second load of sorrow back to the cemetery on the hillside overlooking the glen. Deirdre and Con felt bruised. It was unprofessional to get so involved, but hell, they were human. They took their humanity to the dock behind the restaurant in Rockaway.

"Charles S. Parnell." Deirdre was disgusted. "That damn judge said, 'I realize, Agent Donodio, that the use of this name may rouse suspicion when it is taken in conjunction with the use of the name Oscar Wilde. But this, of itself, is not prima facie evidence that would justify my granting a warrant to search the premises.' "

"It's the law," Con pointed out.

"Dad is furious."

"Well, there's nothing we can do about it. My money's on Morrissey or Garrity. Garrity's disappeared, and we've never been able to find Morrissey. Sooner or later it will catch up with one or both of them. Meanwhile"—he draped an arm covered in impeccable Irish linen about her shoulders—"if you would like to vent a few tears of maidenly frustration on my shoulder, I would be happy to accommodate you."

"Really, Con," she protested even as she was burrowing closer into the proffered shoulder, "I'm not a weepy female who needs consolation."

The moon cooperated, making a shining path across the water. High tide masked the unseemly odors that came when the bottom was exposed. The bridge made a dramatic sweep across the water, highlighted against the glow of lower Manhattan. Con drew her closer and whispered in her ear.

"How are your peptides?"

"My what?"

"Your peptides, or, to be more specific, your oxytocin?"

"I didn't know I had any. What's oxytocin when it's at home?"

"It's a very fine thing given us by the good Lord. It's the hormone that governs our urge to cuddle."

"Good heavens." Deirdre straightened up. "It sounds like a cure for diarrhea."

"There was an article about it in the *Times* a while ago. All kinds of scientific interest. I won't go into all the unseemly details, but I think I have a large supply working right now." He pulled her close again. "Deirdre, forget about the Sullivans for a minute. Will you marry me?"

"But we've known each other for such a short time. Why, I don't even know what your real first name is."

"Never mind my real name, woman. This is serious. I've known you all my life. I just met you a little while ago." He turned her head gently and whispered.

"I don't want a 'relationship.' I don't want an affair. I want you to be my wife. I want you to walk down the aisle at St. Enda's on your father's arm with the pipers to pipe you in, so the whole world will know that we take each other in the sight of God. Please say yes."

It felt right, it was right. She did not believe in quarreling with an idea whose time had come. Looking him straight in the eye, Deirdre said, "Yes." She closed her eyes and waited, breathless, for his confirming kiss.

102

"Whooeee!" Con's yell brought the owner rushing out to the dock.

"Is everything all right? Con, for God's sake, I didn't see you come in. What's all the racket about?"

"She said yes!" He grabbed Deirdre around the waist and waltzed her around the dock.

"This calls for a celebration." Grinning all over his round, bearded face, the restaurateur led them inside. "Drinks for everyone on the house," he ordered. "What's her name?"

"Deirdre, I'd like you to meet Mike Phelan, a wild Rockaway Irishman and a dear friend. Mike, this is Deirdre Donodio, who is as bright as she is beautiful."

When the drinks were served, Mike climbed up on the bar and raised his glass. "Ladies and gentlemen, let us drink to the happiness of Deirdre and Con, who have just agreed to a merger, though the papers are not yet signed. May the road rise up to meet them. May the wind be always at their backs, may the sun shine on their fields, may they see their children's children to the third and fourth generation, and, when their long day draws to its close, may they die in Ireland."

Everyone rose to drink the toast. It was a perfect moment, the kind that etches on the memory to be brought out and relived again and again. But another perfection was added. As the glasses clinked and the applause started, a young fellow who had been sitting behind the bar blew softly into the bagpipes he had been cleaning. The crowd hushed as the haunting strains of that tenderest of Irish love songs, "The Snowy Breasted Pearl," filled the room.

It was nearly midnight when the party broke up. They went silently to the car, afraid to speak and banish the magic. They were on Woodhaven Boulevard when Con cleared his throat.

"What now?"

Deirdre had been waiting for him to speak. She had her answer all ready. "What do you say to checking out each other's peptides?" She flicked a sideways glance.

103

A light changed to red in front of them. Con was so startled he stepped on the gas instead of the brake and nearly rear-ended a blue and white directly in front of them. The blue and white promptly waved them over.

Deirdre burst out laughing as the uniforms approached. Con snapped, "Quiet!" but that set her off even harder. She covered her face and tried to hold it in. Gurgles puffed out around her palms till she sounded like an engine building up steam. He rolled down his window.

"May I see your license, sir?" The uniform, a large black man with a skeptical eye, held out a shovel-size hand. He glanced, did a double take.

"I'm sorry, Sergeant . . ."

"Nothing to be sorry for. You were quite right to stop me." Next to him, Deirdre was subsiding to muffled snorts. She dropped her hands and reached for a tissue to mop her streaming eyes.

"Is everything all right? I mean . . ."—he hesitated delicately—"er . . . do you need some help with the lady?"

"Thank you, no. We're a little excited. We got engaged tonight. For some reason, being pulled over has tickled her funny bone."

A big grin swept over the uniform's face. "Congratulations, Sergeant, and you too, miss. But watch it, it could have been a nasty accident. A pity to spoil the wedding." He closed his notebook and favored them with a friendly leer. "Have a good night."

Con put the car in gear. "Shall we?"

"Shall we what?"

"Have a good night?"

"My place."

It had been a very good night. It was a very good morning. But duty called. They had the day shift.

Deirdre floated in from the kitchen with a steaming cup of coffee. "Time to get up. Even though you still haven't told me your first name, you'll be pleased to know you passed my mother's test."

"And that is?"

"When she was telling me what every young girl should know, she said, '... and remember, dear, a gentleman always supports his weight on his elbows.' "

Con choked. A mouthful of coffee sprayed all over her.

22

MAUREEN'S MURDER WAS on the back burner. Deirdre and Con were deep in wedding plans and new cases. The success of "Grandmother's House" with all the TV and magazine coverage had brought Maire more work than she could handle. She'd hired a secretary to deal with the correspondence and the billing. Brian had benefited, too. If you call it a benefit, he thought sourly. Every day brought a new batch of invitations to speak at this or that garden club, to head up this or that tour, to be interviewed for this or that magazine.

By day he labored to bring the garden to its peak of perfection for the planned September wedding. In the evening, if he wasn't speaking somewhere, he was hosting dinner parties or going to dinner parties for the happy couple. He wasn't sleeping well. In the small hours he sat brooding in the kitchen in his pajamas with Smith on his lap.

Smith was partial to being scratched in a particular spot behind her right ear. Her contented rumble was a pleasing accompaniment to the ticking of the kitchen clock. Brian scratched assiduously as he brooded on the conversation he'd had with Con earlier in the evening. For once there had been no guests, just the four of them.

Maire and Deirdre were deep in technical matters. Words like *peau de soie* and *alençon* salted their conversation. Brian looked at Con and shrugged. He shifted his chair so he wouldn't interrupt the women.

"Let's go to my study and have a drink."

When they were settled, Brian behind his desk and Con in the recliner, each nursing a shot of single malt, Brian looked into his glass as though seeking inspiration.

"It's strange. Deirdre is the last to marry. Maire and I feel as though a chapter in our lives is ending. Tell me, how do you feel about her job?"

"I don't like it. I know there's nothing I can do about it; times have changed, but I still don't think women should be cops." Con stuck out his chin belligerently. "Go ahead, tell me I'm a chauvinist."

"Not me, I feel the same way. My head tells me I'm wrong, but, dammit, my heart goes in the other direction."

"Yeah. Maybe our kids won't have these hang-ups."

"I hope not. It was brought home to me when Maire decided to go back to school and finish her degree. I'd always had the ego to think she was perfectly happy running the house and taking care of me and the kids, but I was wrong. And look what she's made of herself—more clients than she can handle, museums lining up for her to design exhibits. All that talent and drive being held under. It's a crime."

"I know. I hear you, but I don't hear you. It's different with Maire. What she does isn't dangerous. Know what I mean?"

"I know. Just so you know she's an adult and treat her like one. It will all work out."

Brian finished his drink and set the glass down. "I'm glad that's over. When you two have kids of your own you'll have these talks when they get engaged, even though the kids will go right ahead and do what they're going to do regardless. I think one of the hardest things is realizing that someone whose diapers you changed is an adult. And you'll hate sounding like a pompous old fool just as much as I do.

"To change the subject, what's happening about Maureen? Have you given up on her?"

"You know the book is never closed on murder. But we haven't anything definite yet. Our best hope is what the computer people turn up, and that's going to take some time."

"And in the meantime?"

"In the meantime, it's a big city and people get killed every day. It's only in books that a detective can give his whole time to one case. That's the way it is."

Brian shifted Smith, who had discovered an interesting hole in his pajamas and was exploring it with kneading paws. The time had come to redeem his promise. He could give full time to the case. "What about it, Smith? Do you think I should go to Ireland?"

"Rmm, rmm," Smith answered.

"Thanks for agreeing. I think I should go too. This mess started in Ireland and I think that's where I'll find the answers." He spread out a brochure that had arrived in the mail advertising a garden tour of the British Isles and the Irish Republic. He pointed to one item on the itinerary. "See that, Smith? That's where I'm going to start."

23

CON STOOD ASIDE to let Deirdre in. It was the first time she had seen his half of the Chelsea brownstone he shared with his mother and sister. She had, of course, seen his mother's half several times at obligatory prenuptial entertainments, but Con had always sidestepped bringing her upstairs. Two days ago she had laid down the law.

"The wedding is in six weeks and counting. I've given my landlord notice. Don't you think I'm entitled to see where I'm going to live?" She had a point.

For the next two days (his days off) Con had been mysteriously unavailable. The afternoon of the second day he resurfaced on the telephone.

"Dinner tonight at my place?"

"I thought you'd never ask."

The living room stretched across the front of the house. One wall was solid with books, neatly arranged and dusted, with only a few telltale cobwebs still lurking in the corners of the shelves. The sparkling casements sported sheer panels of white voile bisected with the creases of packaging. Flanking the fireplace were two well-used and comfortable armchairs, one occupied by an elderly Irish setter that gave a token bark before she climbed painfully down to greet them.

"This is Medb. Shake hands, Medb."

Courtesies were gravely offered and accepted.

Con threw open another door. "This was meant to be the dining room, but I put it to other uses." A ballet barre ran the full length of the mirrored inside wall. Exercise equipment was bunched at the far end.

"What on earth . . . ?"

He sounded defensive. "There's a group of us in the department. We do ballet. It's more fun than regular exercise. There's a fellow from the American Ballet Theater who gives us lessons now and again."

"I think it's wonderful. Do you ever dance in public?"

"Sometimes. We call ourselves the Corps de Cops. We were in a thing a couple of years ago at Madison Square Garden. We were warrior princes in a pageant."

"But why so elaborate a setup?"

"Well, I have the space and the other guys come up here to practice. When we're doing a show and all have to rehearse together, we use one of the PAL gyms."

"Con, I love you. How did I get so lucky? Where's the kitchen? And, by the way, what do the initials H.V. stand for on the wedding invitations?"

"You'll find out soon enough about the initials. And you may not think you're so lucky when you see the kitchen. This way."

Well, thought Deirdre, wrinkling her nose, at least it's large, and I love the stove. The stove stood on four legs, all pale cream enamel with light green trim. The oven on the side was at standing height with a warming shelf above and a broiler below. Her words followed her thought. "I love the stove, I've always wanted one like that. It's older than the two of us put together. Does it work?"

"It works."

"Great. We'll keep it. But that one-legged sink has to go, and the ratty linoleum, and the refrigerator. Maybe we could donate it to a museum. We'll keep the cabinets. They'll be great refinished. I love this place. What's upstairs?"

"This was all one house when my great-grandfather bought it. Upstairs were the servants' rooms. Now it's four bedrooms."

"Lead on. Your great-grandfather?"

They were climbing a narrow stair. "Back in 1914. He raised twelve kids and didn't have any servants, but they sure filled the bedrooms. He was a police captain when Teddy Roosevelt was commissioner."

He pushed open the first door off the narrow landing. The room revealed was low ceilinged under slanting eaves. A huge brass bedstead facing a narrow grate for a coal fire took up half of the floor.

"Very nice."

"Want to try it?"

"Later, you sex fiend."

There were three more smaller rooms. Two empty, the third with a desk and personal computer.

"This is my office."

"Office?"

"Well, you know. Taxes and records. And I write a little."

"Con Connolly, I've found out more about you in the last half hour than I knew when I agreed to marry you."

He grabbed her from behind. "Life is one fantastic voyage of discovery. Think of all the things I don't know about you yet. How about we go next door and discover a few things about each other?"

"Unhand me, villain. I'm hungry. Besides, your mother and sister are downstairs trying to figure out what we're doing from the noises, or lack of them. Let's go down and give them some nice to and fro from the kitchen."

"You're a cruel and unfeeling wench."

"And you're a slavering monster."

"Did you know that's from the Icelandic *slafra* and has a variety of meanings, all of them related and unpleasant?"

"No, I didn't. And I find your store of knowledge about slavering highly suspect."

"How so?"

"Takes one to know one."

"Let's slaver together, my little Grendel."

"Thanks a heap. I'll say something nice about you some-day. What's for dinner?"

She marched firmly down the stairs and settled herself at the small table laid for two between the windows in the living room. Medb wheezed over and planted herself at tidbit alert.

Con called from the kitchen, "Would you like a glass of wine before we eat? I have a Chablis that the fellow in the liquor store tells me is the very best. I'm not much of a judge, so I took his word. Want to try?"

"If you'll come in and drink with me. And bring something for Medb."

"She knows better than to eat from the table. She's just taking advantage." He poured the wine carefully into two Waterford glasses.

"Waterford?"

"These are Mom's. She said I had nothing decent up here with which to entertain my future wife. The china's hers too."

"How about the silver and linen?"

"Guilty."

Deirdre took a sip. "Mmm, that's good. I'm so glad they're hers. I'd much rather start with our own things." She set down her glass. "Con, I'm worried about Dad."

"What's he up to now?"

"This trip he's planning to Ireland. I'm afraid he's going to get into trouble. This time we won't be around to bail him out."

"You think he was lying about going to relax and look at gardens?"

"No, he never lies. He just doesn't tell the whole truth. He'll tour his precious gardens to salve his conscience, then

112

he'll hotfoot it up to Donegal and start poking around in . . . what was the name of that town?"

"Two towns, if I remember correctly. Ballyglenfoyle and Portnoo."

"Well, there's nothing we can do to stop him. But he's not leaving for three weeks, and anything can happen in that length of time. Let's not let it spoil our evening."

Good smells were coming from the suspiciously neat kitchen. "You sit tight. I'll just go and check my cooking."

"Whose cooking? That kitchen looked awfully neat."

"Oh, all right, if you must know. Mother cooked."

Indeed she had. There was vichyssoise followed by a black bean and goat's cheese salad flavored with just a hint of fresh dill and an assortment of farm-fresh vegetables.

"You know Mother's a vegetarian," Con apologized.

"I would be too, if I could turn out a meal like this." Deirdre stirred her cup of freshly ground coffee and sat back. "Con, I think I'm going to quit the INS."

A great gladness swelled up in Con's heart, but he was clever enough not to let it show. "Why?"

"Lots of reasons. I can see it making a lot of trouble between us; they can assign me anywhere, while you have to stay in New York. But the main reason is . . ."—she paused, trying to find the right words—"the people we go after usually aren't criminals, except technically. They're just poor devils trying to find a better life for themselves and their families. I just don't want to do it any longer."

Con pushed back from the table. "Let's go into the living room and talk it over. Have you any idea what you might want to do instead?" He plumped down in one of the old leather chairs and pulled her down on his lap.

"Something to do with police work. I should have stood up against Dad and insisted on taking the NYPD test. Then we wouldn't have this problem. I never wanted to be anything but a cop." She burrowed her head into his neck. "You're such a blessed comfort."

"We aim to please."

For a little while Con gave all of his attention to just that. "You don't have to decide anything today, you know, except one thing."

"What's that?"

"I think we should check out the mattress upstairs and see if you like it. If we have to buy a new one it will take a few weeks to be delivered."

24

BRIAN SETTLED BACK into his seat on the big green-and-blue Aer Lingus jet. He'd done it. Getting away had not been easy.

"But it's so close to the wedding," Maire and Deirdre had objected in one voice.

"I'll be back in plenty of time. Between work and planning, I've just been a nuisance under your feet for the last month. The garden's fine. The Gomez boy is coming in every day to water and weed. He's got the makings of a fine gardener."

"I hope you're not planning to do anything silly," Con said with a meaningful glance at Deirdre.

"I wasn't able to do much in New York, where I know my way around. What on earth could I do in Ireland? No, I need some time to myself, and I want to go and look at gardens." Maire looked wistful. "Next time, my dear, we'll both go. You know you can't get away now."

Brian hated flying almost as much as Deirdre did. But if he had to fly, Aer Lingus was the airline he trusted most. He'd never heard of its having a fatal accident, and he was not afraid of terrorist sabotage—the IRA would never stand for it. Besides, it named its planes for the Irish saints. Knowing that the Atlantic was thirty-five thousand feet below was a little easier to take when you cowered in the belly of *St. Brendan*.

Nevertheless, when they turned for takeoff and the engine decibels rose to manic fury, he felt a thrill from chest to groin and his hands gripped the armrests. The upward thrust against his legs and the pressure of the seat belt did little for his peace of mind. By the time he decided that they weren't going to blow up, drop like a stone, or disappear into some other dimension, he was already over the ocean and committed to the course he had so vehemently disowned to Con. Not that he thought Con believed him for a minute when he claimed to be interested only in gardens. However, . . .

The seat belt light winked off. The lassies of Aer Lingus limbered up the drinks trolley. Brian glanced at the seat mate he had ignored during the terrors of takeoff. A small man, everything about him neat and dapper. Black hair slicked straight back, reminiscent of a 1920s gigolo. A truly magnificent nose jutting out between black eyebrow hedges to overhang a bushy mustache. Who did he know who had a nose like that? Smaller but definitely blade shaped? His suit had never seen a rack; it shrieked Savile Row. He thought ruefully of his own spring sale outfit from Macy's and shrugged.

The man smiled. "I hate takeoffs. My whole life passes before me."

A sensible fellow. "Me too," Brian confessed. "I always promise my guardian angel that I'll be good for the rest of my life."

"What are you drinking?"

"Bushmill's and soda."

The flight attendant was waiting. "Make that two."

"Your first trip to Ireland?"

"No, but it's been several years."

"On holiday?"

"I'm escaping." Brian lowered his voice dramatically. "My daughter's getting married in September. Every room is full of things I mustn't touch. My wife's conversation has become incomprehensible. They keep nagging at me about getting the garden in top shape for the reception, though the poor plants are already groomed within an inch of their lives. So I told them enough is enough and hopped a plane. Brian Donodio," he added, holding out his hand.

"Turlough McSwiggan. I have a bit of a garden myself. You're not *the* Brian Donodio, are you?"

"The only one I know of." Brian fortified himself with a swallow. "Why do you ask?"

"I read an article about your garden in Woodside. I'd hoped to be able to get out and pay it a visit, but I couldn't fit it in on this trip. The pictures are beautiful."

The PA system clicked on. "This is Captain Daugherty speaking. We're running into just a little turbulence out here and we'll be going up a bit to get on top of it. If you'll fasten your seat belts and sit tight we should be over it very soon."

Brian survived the rough weather and the dinky plastic dinner. As time wore on he even found himself less alert to the beat of the engines. Turlough McSwiggan was proving himself an ideal seatmate When *St. Brendan* started its final approach to Shannon Airport the two had the beginning of a friendship.

"I'm going on to Dublin later." McSwiggan fumbled in his wallet. "Here's my card. If you find a few hours hanging heavy, give me a call and I'll show off my little garden. I put my Dublin address and telephone on the back." He gathered his hand luggage and stepped into the aisle.

Brian turned the bit of pasteboard over. "Consultant" was inscribed below McSwiggan's name. I wonder, he thought, what he consults about and if he is always this friendly?

Not many were taking the hop-skip-and-jump flight to Dublin. In less than a half hour Brian looked down at a herd of cows peacefully grazing on the verge of the capital's runway.

117

25

WHEN IN IRELAND, Brian always stayed at a bed and breakfast on Clontarf Road. Over the years Maire and he had become very fond of Mrs. Molloy, the landlady.

"Dr. Donodio, you're looking grand. I'm sorry Mrs. Donodio couldn't come."

"And I'm sorry too. But our Deirdre is getting married in September and she didn't feel she could get away."

"Isn't that grand. I've put you in the front room, the one overlooking the bay."

"Wonderful." He lifted his bag to go upstairs. The house had not changed. Impeccably clean, totally comfortable, and furnished with the most god-awful collection of overstuffed furniture. Years ago he and Maire had stayed at a B and B a few doors down, whose landlady was so insufferably genteel, they had hated to flush. They were sure Mrs. Fitzmaurice acknowledged nothing so crude as bodily functions.

Escaping early one morning for a walk, Brian had spotted Mrs. Molloy working in her garden and stopped to admire and chat. On learning that she too ran a B and B, he flung himself on her mercy, then ran to collect Maire and the luggage. And so a tradition was born.

When Brian came down, keyed up and tired at the same time with jet lag, Mrs. Molloy greeted him with a cup of tea.

"Now you just sit and be comfortable for a minute while you get yourself together, then you can tell me all the news. You'll be pleased to know that the roses this year at St. Anne's are outdoing themselves."

St. Anne's Rose Garden was one of the reasons for choosing Clontarf Road as his Irish base. The other reason was its proximity to the botanic gardens. He settled back and sipped his tea. This trip garden tours were only his cover. Maybe he could start the ball rolling with Mrs. Molloy.

All of the news was exchanged. Brian cleared his throat and continued, "One more thing. Was there much in the papers here about the murder in New York of Ban Garda Maureen Sullivan?"

"Indeed there was. And wasn't it a terrible thing? My cousin Jim, who's in the Garda, was just talking about it the other day."

"Your cousin?"

"Superintendent, he is. And he was after telling me that he himself knew Maureen. A lovely person, he said. When I told him you'd called that you were coming over, he got all excited. Your name is well known now here in Ireland."

"I had no idea."

"Yes indeed. He says headquarters is still working round the clock to help the Yanks find out who did it."

"I'd like to meet your cousin." Brian reflected that one of the advantages of a small country was that everyone always had a cousin somewhere who was close to the heart of things.

"And he'd be glad to make your acquaintance."

Brian told her of his involvement, omitting his real purpose. She sighed pleasurably when he told of the romance between Deirdre and Con.

"It's just like a story." Sentimental moisture glazed her eyes. "And to think that wee girl of yours is in the police herself. Well, good luck to them. I'll call Jim on the telephone and tell him. We'll fix something up. Now, what are your plans?"

"Fine days like this are too good to waste. I'm going to take a walk up to St. Anne's to see the roses, then coming back here to sleep."

Half a mile's brisk walk brought him to the rose garden, where the display was, indeed, very fine. But his mind was not on the flowers. He had no authority, and no idea of where to begin his quest for the truth. All he had was the elusive smell and the fact, which might have no bearing whatever on the case, that Patrick Garrity seemed to have disappeared.

Perhaps Mrs. Molloy's cousin might prove the entrée he needed. It was somewhat like a John Buchan thriller. What would Richard Hannay have done? In *The Thirty-nine Steps* there had been a master criminal. He turned the idea over in his mind.

He knew that the INS and the NYPD had been working on the assumption that the killings and the computer juggling were IRA connected. Now he found himself questioning this assumption. It didn't smell right. There must be a huge amount of money to be made in selling phony green cards, and the ramifications were enormous. Drugs? Maybe he would pass the idea on to Deirdre when he called home. No, she'd just laugh in that smug way she had and tell him to leave it to the professionals. Well, the professionals hadn't done much to write home about.

A German shepherd came running to his bench, sat down in front of him, and gravely offered its paw. Brian shook it. "How do you do, sir, or madam, as the case may be?"

A man, obviously the dog's master, to judge by the leash dangling from his hand, sat down next to Brian. Tweed cap, needed a haircut, shiny brown suit, scars from adolescent acne. The prevailing smell was Guinness. In New York Brian would have moved away, but this was Dublin.

"Beautiful dog."

"I hope he's not bothering you. Name's Tinker."

"Nice to know you, Tinker."

"You're a Yank," the man exclaimed as though making a rare discovery.

"I'm an American, yes."

"On holiday, then?"

"Yes. I'm planning to see the Irish gardens." Brian yawned and shook his head. "Excuse me. I just got here this morning. I guess the time difference is catching up with me." He rose. "Good-bye, Tinker. Nice to have met you."

The man rose with him. "I'll walk to the road with you. Can't be too careful these days. St. Anne's is lonely and Dublin is full of tearaways."

"Very civil of you."

Instead of the long way out through the landscaped entrance, the man led Brian to a dank little archway through the stone wall surrounding the garden.

"This way's shorter." The fellow was too close.

Brian's New York reflexes screamed into action, but it was too late. He felt his jacket screw up in a mighty grip as he slammed into the stone of the arch. Tinker changed into a growling, fanged monster. The man's face thrust within an inch of his own.

"This time it's only a warning. Take the next plane back. We don't welcome bloody Yanks sticking their big noses in where they don't belong." His fist flashed back and dealt Brian a crushing blow in the diaphragm, sending his breath from his lungs in a great whoosh. He bent over double, clutching his belly and groping for his spectacles, praying they had not been broken when they flew from his nose. A kick from the rear sent him sprawling on his knees. When he was able to straighten up, the man had gone.

26

APART FROM A sore gut, there didn't seem to be much damage.
He retrieved his glasses and settled his clothes. The man had
been telling the truth about the arch. It led him right out to
the road and the reassurance of busy traffic. From now on
he'd stick to peopled areas. Easy enough in Dublin, but
difficult when he got to Donegal. He considered calling the
Garda and reporting the incident, but he decided against it.
He would have to tell the whole story and they would warn
him off. Right now, bed was the next stop.

"Did your friend catch up with you?"

"My friend?"

"Young fellow with a beautiful dog. Came looking about
a half hour after you left. He didn't look quite your type, but
they all look like unmade beds these days. I hope it was all
right for me to tell him where to find you."

"He caught up with me. You might say we had an explo-
sive meeting."

Without explanation, he mounted the stairs and threw
himself on the bed. Sleep would not come. Who knew where
he was staying in Dublin besides his family? He'd put the
address on his landing card, but those were probably still in

a pile somewhere waiting to be entered in a computer when someone had nothing better to do. He'd told Turlough McSwiggan that he was staying at a B and B on Clontarf Road, but he was sure he hadn't mentioned Mrs. Molloy's name. One thing was sure, he was on some kind of a trail, even if he couldn't see it himself yet. With this realization he relaxed and fell asleep.

When he woke his watch told him he had slept for more than six hours. He was stiff, his stomach hurt. He was also ravenously hungry. He thought regretfully of the room service he could have commanded if he'd stayed at the Shelbourne, reminded himself of the money he was saving by not staying there, and grabbed his coat to go out and hunt up a local eatery. He seemed to remember a small fish and chips place a few blocks away.

Mrs. Molloy intercepted him. "I called my cousin Jimmy, the garda, and asked him over for a bite and to meet you. It being your first day and all, I thought you might prefer to eat here."

Wonderful woman! "That's very kind, Mrs. Molloy. I would be honored."

Cousin Jimmy was an enormous man, six feet four in his socks and broad. He enfolded Brian's hand carefully in his huge paw and stared down with shrewd blue eyes under bristling brows matched by a truly magnificent James Connolly mustache.

"Welcome to Ireland, Dr. Donodio. Nuala here has often told me of you and your wife."

This was the first time Brian had penetrated to Mrs. Molloy's private quarters. The minuscule living room was dominated by a huge TV set and the table was set in the larger kitchen, near to the stove (or cooker, as the Irish called it). And it was not meanly set. There was fresh broiled salmon, tiny new potatoes, asparagus cooked just enough that the tough was gone but the crunch was there, and a magnificent apple tart topped with fresh cream. A meal for the gods.

He pushed back from the table satisfied but not sated.

"Mrs. Molloy, that was a memorable meal. I think it's the best I've ever eaten."

"Get on with you, now. That's a fine thing to be saying. I'm sure Mrs. Donodio has fed you many a better."

"Let's go into the lounge and have a sup." Cousin Jimmy pushed back from the table. "We'll be out of Nuala's way while she washes up." An interesting bottle of single malt appeared and the two men settled back.

"Now, Nuala was telling me that you wanted to talk to me about finding poor Maureen's body."

"Yes." Brian knew he had to trust someone in Ireland, and who better than this gentle Garda giant. He told the whole story, ending with his experience of the morning at St. Anne's.

There was a moment's silence when he finished. Jimmy shook his head. "I'd tell you to go straight home, except I know you won't. I agree with your daughter and Sergeant Connolly. You should leave this to the professionals."

"So far the professionals have struck out."

Jimmy held out his hand. "Let me wet that drink for you. What makes you think you'll have better luck?"

"The fact that I was warned off this morning."

"Next time they may do more than warn you. What are your plans while you're here?"

"Tomorrow the botanic gardens, and I'll visit a few book-stores in the city. I want to stop by Trinity and salute the Book of Kells. Then I'm going to Powerscourt, Mount Usher, and the Japanese Gardens at the National Stud."

"Why those places?"

"I'm supposed to be looking at gardens."

"And you shall. What I suggest is going to Donegal first and doing what you have to do, no matter what anyone says. Then you can take some pleasure in the gardens."

Brian rolled the matter over in his mind. "I'll be in just as much danger in Donegal, if what you say is true."

"No you won't." Jimmy smiled with satisfaction. "I'm going with you."

124

"You're what?"

"I have a few days' leave due me. Maureen was my friend, and I think you're on to something, or they think you are, which is just as good. I won't ask permission, they'd only tell me no."

They planned an early start for the north. Brian knew he was in for a long night. All he had was hints, surmises, and the clear indication that he was on to something. He wished he knew what that something was. Time to put down what he knew and what he guessed. Set it all down on paper. He took a yellow pad from his briefcase and propped himself up on the bed.

1. Monica Sullivan comes to the U.S. on a tourist visa, but the INS computer shows that she has a green card. She disappears.
2. There is no paperwork to back up the green card in either the U.S. or Ireland.
3. Maureen Sullivan takes her annual leave to try and find out what became of Monica.
4. Maureen indicates to Deirdre that she is very troubled, but would not give any hard information.
5. Maureen asks for my help. I get there too late.
6. After Maureen was killed, someone laid her out on the couch and placed a rosary in her hands. (But the bastard didn't think of the flies. Almost more than the killing, I hate him because of the flies.)
7. The apartment loaned to Maureen in Chelsea is rented under the name of "Oscar Wilde."
8. There is a smell in the Chelsea apartment I cannot identify, but I have smelled it before.
9. Barney Finucane drinks and sniffs coke. He has a reputation as a womanizer. He gets terribly upset when I ask him about the fancy computer setup at the center.

10. Barney Finucane lives in New Rumple in an apartment rented under "Charles S. Parnell."

11. It is on the hillside near his apartment that Monica Sullivan's body is found.

12. Barney Finucane is found shot at his desk at the center, with a note confessing to the murders of Maureen, Monica, and myself. His murder is fixed to look like suicide. I smell the same odor in Barney's office that I smelled in Maureen's apartment.

13. Shortly before he is found he calls me, saying he has to speak to me and it cannot wait until morning.

14. Two masked figures rush out of the center just before the discovery of Barney's body.

15. Sean Morrissey (probably not his real name) claims Maureen was his girlfriend. He refuses to give me his address and there is no record of his being in the country legally. The Four Green Fields is under observation as a gathering place for illegals.

16. Patrick Garrity comes from Portnoo near Ballyglenfoyle and knows the Sullivan family. Barney and he are sweating and uneasy when they come to "To Grandmother's House We Go."

17. Patrick Garrity has an alibi for Maureen's murder but the Boston police say not to trust it. Following Barney's murder he disappears, though he is a legal immigrant and is not a particular suspect.

18. According to Deirdre and Con, the INS is checking all green cards. They fear that the problem spreads far beyond Ireland.

Brian sat back and considered. It was all a lot of smoke and shadow, but the corpses were very real. He took a clean sheet and wrote MAYBE across the top in big black letters.

1. Deirdre, Con, and everyone else from Land's End to Timbuktu are of the opinion that this is an IRA

operation. I don't agree. Doesn't smell right. I think this is straightforward (if I can use the word) criminality. I think there's a mastermind at work, hoping the IRA will be blamed. Drugs? International traffic in phony green cards? (Have I been reading too much John Buchan?)

2. How did Turlough McSwiggan just happen to be on the same flight and seat I was on? From his clothes I'd have expected him to fly first class. On the other hand, it could be a coincidence and he may just be of the "back end of the plane gets there the same time as the front end" school. (Note: Call McSwiggan in A.M. to say I'm heading north.)

3. How about Mrs. Molloy's cousin Jimmy? It seems very convenient that he's able to take a few days off just like that. Too convenient?

4. Why didn't the fellow who attacked me this morning just go ahead and finish the job?

His watch read 2:30. He still wasn't sleepy. Shoes in hand, he slipped down the stairs and let himself out of the house. No great city is ever entirely silent, but daytime noise was muted to a barely discernible mutter. He crossed the road to lean on the sea wall overlooking Dublin Bay. The tide was in, reflecting a million stars and the light of a three-quarters moon. To his right was the dark silhouette of North Bull Island, to his left one of southern Ireland's incongruous palm trees flourishing by courtesy of the Gulf Stream.

He shivered suddenly, though the night was mild. His mother would have told him that a goose walked over his grave. He turned to meet the mild gaze of a blue-coated, blue-capped garda.

"Is anything wrong, sir?"

"I felt the wings of Azrael."

"I hear him often at this hour, though I'm more like to think it's the wailing of the *bean-sidhe*. Fancies come easily in the early hours. Are you staying near here?"

127

"Across the street."

"Then I'd be inside, if I were you. I'll watch you in. Sad to say, but it's not safe out here anymore."

"It's safer here than most places. Good night, officer."

The reason was obscure, but he felt comforted. Now he could sleep.

27

COUSIN JIMMY ARRIVED with the day to share a huge Irish breakfast. Porridge thick enough to hold the spoon upright, with real cream. Farm-cured bacon, fresh eggs, whole-meal bread, and pots of strong tea. A cholesterol lover's feast. Brian ate every bite. His night terrors and suspicions were gone with the strong sunshine.

He pushed back from the table. "Delicious, Mrs. Molloy. Don't hurry over your tea, Costigan"—for that was Jimmy's surname—"I have a few more things to pack and some calls to make."

Mrs. Molloy came to the door to see them off. "I spoke to Maire," Brian said. "She sends you her regards and hopes to see you soon."

"Have a good journey."

Jimmy drove a late model Ford sedan. Brian sat in the passenger seat, battling his leaping heart as the oncoming traffic swept down from the wrong side. As they sped north on the N3 he started to settle down. Fine weather raised a holiday spirit in spite of his grim errand. Farmers were in the fields, cutting and baling hay. Washing hung in banners on the lines. Younger children played, older ones worked beside their parents. Cows and horses grazed the lush meadows, and half-grown lambs gamboled beside their mothers. On a day such as this, who could believe in black evil?

Jimmy was a good companion, pointing out sights, explaining, adding items of local lore. Brian listened with half an ear. When they left Mrs. Molloy's he noticed a gray Citroen pull out from the curb behind them. He thought nothing of it at the time, but now he noticed the same car. He was sure it was the same.

"We're being followed."

Jimmy took a quick glance. "You're mistaken, I think. There's a lot of motors on the N3."

"I'd agree with you, but that car was waiting outside your cousin's house, and now it's here."

"I'm not disagreeing with you, mind. Let's turn off into this side road and see if he follows."

The car sped past without slowing. "See, just some fellow on his way north, the same as we. Since we turned off here, would you like to make a side trip to Tara?"

Brian was embarrassed. "Sorry. I guess I'm seeing spooks. Yes, I'd love to stop at Tara. It's one of my favorite places."

There were no buses at the tourist center. "Great," Jimmy remarked. "We have the place to ourselves except for the sheep. Don't wait for me, I'll catch up. I hate these damn centers, but they're a wonderful relief to the kidneys."

Brian was happy to wander alone. The Hill of Tara is not to be appreciated in company. A man alone can meet the ghosts of Ireland's past . . . relive the great feasts and gatherings . . . see Patrick kindle the Easter fire on the Hill of Slane . . . "No more to chiefs and ladies bright . . ." Lost in his romantic musings on past glories that had little relation to historical fact, he stooped to look through the iron bars at the cut-away interior of the Hill of Hostages, a megalithic burial mound. When excavated it contained not only funerary urns full of ashes but the body of a young man with a necklace of faience, bronze, and amber. He often remembered the young

130

man in his prayers. It was sad to find two beer cans and a fish and chips wrapper thrust through the bars.

Brian straightened with annoyance just as something whistled past him to bury itself in the turf of the mound, where his head had been only a moment before.

Skills buried deep in his subconscious since World War II came roaring back to life. He hurled himself down to one side and lay gripping the turf, his nose buried in sheep droppings.

Moments later feet came pounding up the hill. "Man, are you all right? I was just coming up to join you when I saw you drop like a stone."

Brian rolled over and sat up, wrinkling his nose at the ripe odor of his suit. "I'm fine. Someone took a pot shot and missed."

"They never . . ."

"Oh, yes they did," Brian's face was grim. He dug out his pen knife and probed the mound. "See?" The bullet lay in his palm, still warm. "If I hadn't stood when I did, you could have popped me right in there with the other bodies."

"It's not as bad as all that," Jimmy soothed, "the bugger missed you. And now that he sees there's two of us, he won't try again."

Brian wasn't so sure; his antennae were quivering at Jimmy's unpolicemanlike attitude. "It was attempted murder; shouldn't we call the Garda?"

"Well, look at it this way. If we call the local men, we'll be here for hours argy-bargying back and forth while the wee devil slips through our fingers. Let's go find you a drink, then be on our way. We know we're on to something. Maureen was my friend, I want to be with you when we nail the bastard."

A pub was not hard to find. Two whiskeys later a thought popped into Brian's head. Sixty-five years in New York and he had never been attacked. He had been in peaceful Ireland less than forty-eight hours and this was the second round. He fingered the spent bullet in his pocket and shivered.

28

THE TELEPHONE RANG.

"Hello."

"Missed him," the voice on the other end announced laconically.

"Bugger has a charmed life. We can't afford to miss the next time."

"Don't worry. I'll make sure."

"No. This time *I'll* make sure."

"Whatever you say."

The receiver slammed back with more than necessary force.

"If you want a thing done well, do it yourself, as our American cousins would say." He turned to his companion. "You heard?"

She nodded, like one of those Chinese mandarin statuettes with a tippy head.

"I blame myself," he went on. "The failure in New York was no one's fault. I should have had him finished off at St. Anne's. The trouble is, I like the fellow and only ordered a warning. Never let sentiment get in the way of business." He gave a satisfied nod as though this were an original thought and waited for his audience to agree.

"I still like him. Let's make it quick and clean."

It was rising three o'clock when Jimmy and Brian rounded the corner and entered Ballyglenfoyle's main street. Brian was still upset over his close escape at Tara and troubled over what he privately considered Jimmy's unethical, unpolicelike nonreporting of the incident.

The road north had led through a succession of bleak, stone-built villages with unadorned gray fronts facing the streets, villages that matched his gray mood and gloomy forebodings. Ballyglenfoyle burst upon him like a song, lifting his spirits. Stretched before him were buildings washed in soft color, pink, yellow, white, and blue. Flowers in window boxes relieved the severity of the traditional architecture.

"Now this is something. Drive slowly down the street before we find a hotel. I'd like to see the whole place."

"Why not? It's a pretty place. Won the Tidy Town Award several times."

The main street, bisected by a chuckling river with a plaque to the memory of a local poet on the bridge, led on to a large school set on a hillside. On the corner was a stone grotto with statues of Our Lady of Lourdes appearing to St. Bernadette.

"This is my idea of what an Irish town should be. Where's a good place to stay?"

"Most stay at the Glenfoyle. I've heard the food is very good."

"Lead on, MacDuff."

"Don't say that."

"Why?"

"Remember what happened to him."

"Thanks," Brian said sourly, "I was just starting to enjoy myself."

The lobby of the Glenfoyle was shadowed and cool after the sun. To one side was the lounge, on the other side the pub, which was doing a roaring business. Brian wondered where everyone came from on a workday. Then he realized that this was the height of the holiday season. He just hoped they'd have space available. He advanced on the desk, where a comely young woman was sorting a pile of bills. She put down her papers.

"May I help you?"

"My friend and I would like to stay for a couple of days."

"Would you like a double?"

"Yes," said Jimmy,

"No," said Brian.

"Which is it to be, then?"

"No offense, Jimmy. I know you're a nice fellow, but I'm not very good at this sharing business. Man gets to my time of life, he values his privacy. You understand?" Damn well better, was the unspoken corollary.

"I have one single open, but it doesn't have its own bath. Or I could give you each a double in the new wing with bath. A tour party had to cancel two rooms."

Jimmy spoke quickly. "The single for me."

"Then I'll have the double."

The register was produced. "Will you be eating both meals in then? It's a special rate if you do."

"Yes, I think so. It seems very nice." Brian shouldered his bag and took the proffered key. "I'm going to have a wash; I still smell of the sheep droppings at Tara. Meet you in the pub, okay?"

"Fine. I'll stop by for you in about twenty minutes?"

The stairs behind the desk led up to a broad landing lined with little carrels for letter writing, then on to a long corridor. Brian's room was large, with two double beds covered with matching green spreads. Over the beds was a wooden strip supporting reading lights and a phone jack. The phone itself was missing. He raced back down to the desk and checked that Jimmy was nowhere in earshot.

"May I have a telephone upstairs?"

"Surely, Dr. Donodio. I'll send one right up."

"If you have it here at the counter, I can take it up myself. I know how to plug it in."

"Fine. You're sure it's no trouble, now?"

Back in the room he plugged the phone in to be sure it worked, then disconnected it and hid it in a drawer. When the knock he expected came he was boiling water in the kettle for a cup of tea.

"Come."

"They've done you well. You couldn't swing a cat in my room. Well, what are your plans?"

"Good question. So far things have seemed to come to me, if you catch my meaning. This is the only thing I have planned." He reached inside his bag and pulled out the garden tour brochure that had sparked his quest.

> August 4: Visit to Portnoo Gardens. Ten acres
> designed by Alexander McLeish in the
> "gardenesque" manner in the early 19th century
> under the patronage of the Marquess of
> Coyningham. This little-known gem had practically
> reverted to the wild when it passed into the
> possession of Margaret Garrity in the late 1960s.
> More than 20 years of devoted restoration have
> brought this garden back to its original beauty. In
> the afternoon we will visit the famed
> "Robinsonian" gardens at Glenveagh.

"My plan is to go tomorrow morning when the tour group is there and look things over."

"Why not today?"

"Safety in numbers, I guess. This Margaret Garrity may be pure as snow, and so may her brother Patrick. I met him in New York and he's the only real lead I have. It may all be a mare's nest and I'll discover nothing. At least I'll have tried."

The kettle whistled. "I think I'd rather have a real drink. Shall we go?"

Once they were settled with their pints Brian realized that most of the crowd were tourists, American and English, with German predominating. Children wandered in and out, their faces glued to bottles of Day-Glo orange soda.

"May I join you?" A thin-faced, sandy-haired man in a tweed suit was standing uncertainly by their banquette. There were vacant spots at other tables.

"Our pleasure." Brian moved over.

"Name's Gildea. How do you like Ballyglenfoyle?"

"I'm Donodio, this is Costigan, and we like it fine."

"On holiday?"

"I'm here to visit gardens. I particularly want to see Glen-veagh and Margaret Garrity's at Portnoo. My friend is more interested in fishing." Brian stuck his nose back into his pint and drank up. "Another round?"

The bar was crowded. Brian waited patiently, his long nose quivering as he tried to catalog the smells, untangling each from the general fug. Beer, stout, whiskey. A sharp, smoky tang. Ah, that must be peat burning. He traced an overpowering sweetness mixed with sweat to a fat, blond woman in a too-tight flowered dress. Someone fairly close needed to visit his dentist. It was that ferret-faced fellow with the wispy mustache. That redheaded baby in the stroller needed a clean diaper. Tobacco overlay everything else. Did all the Irish smoke? Patiently he sniffed, sorted, traced each odor to its source.

"What will it be, sir?" Spicy, aromatic, the death scent hit him like a blow. Or was it quite the same?

The open-faced young bartender was waiting. "Three pints, please. Excuse me, I know you're busy, but could you tell me the name of the aftershave you're using and where to buy it?"

"It's called Fianna's Warrior; my girl gave it me for Christmas. Do you like it, then?"

"It's an interesting smell. I'd like to get some to take home."

"Across the street at the co-op, or down this side at the general store. It's made locally. Three pints—here you are, sir."

Finally he had a lead for his nose to follow. He polished off his pint as fast as decency permitted and got up. "I'm going out to explore the town," he told Jimmy. "Don't hurry. I just want to look around."

The co-op store was small and crowded with a bewildering array of goods. Brian's nose led him unerringly to the cosmetics shelf with its array of aftershave, cologne, perfume, lotions, and creams under the Fianna label. Fianna Warrior for men, Fianna Alainn for women. All had basically the same smell. All were manufactured in Donegal. He bought one of each.

Costigan and Gildea were still huddled over their pints. Brian raced up the stairs to his room to sniff his purchases. When his nose dipped into the last bottle a smile of satisfaction and comprehension lighted his face. He remembered where he had smelled the Fianna smell before he found Maureen. When the bottles were carefully stowed away, he plugged in the phone.

"Sullivan? Donodio. I'm here at the Glenfoyle. When can we meet? . . . No, not tonight . . . St. Bride's? . . . tomorrow then . . . give my regards to Grania."

He returned to the pub.

29

BRIAN ROSE EARLY. A lusty vibrato from Jimmy's room testified that his companion was still wrapped in chaste and single slumber.

He walked slowly to the lobby, reflecting that today would be the turning point. His options were narrowing but he still could walk away. He could cancel the trip to Portnoo and the fate he was sure awaited him, for good or ill. By tomorrow either he might have won or he might easily be dead. Death was not his preferred agenda, but as a prudent man he felt he could not discount the possibility. Across the road a few people were entering St. Bride's Church for early mass. He turned to follow them.

It was not actually raining, but the air was more than moist. A sort of heavy, gray condensation that fit his mood. The church was modern. A soaring structure of natural wood, stone, and whitened plaster. It seemed made for sunshine and the song of birds. Inside, his eye was held by a tall stone cross to the side of the altar. A contemporary version of the old Celtic crosses. He bowed his head.

"Give me courage," he prayed, "to do what I have to do," for the temptation was strong to drop his quest. It was what everyone had urged. From the corner of his eye he saw Dualta Sullivan dressed in rough work clothes slip into a side chapel. He joined him.

He was in a state of high excitement. "Man, it's good to see you." He grabbed Brian's hand in a bear grip. "I can't talk long now, I have to get to work. But I'll take tomorrow off and as long as we need. I'm your man."

Brian cast the die. "I'm going down to Portnoo today to see Maggie Garrity. If I don't come back this afternoon I want you to go to the Garda and give them this"—he handed over a thick envelope—"and tell them to get in touch with Con Connolly, you remember him, in New York. Con will know what to do."

"God bless you. I'll be praying for you."

"You do that. Get on to work now. Mass is about to start."

Jimmy waved to him through the dining room window. His traveling companion was a mighty trencherman, piling huge amounts of eggs and gammon rasher on his fork. When Brian came in he motioned him to the seat opposite and spoke through a full mouth.

"Morning, Brian. Pull up a seat and they'll take your order in a minute. Where have you been?"

"Mass."

"Something I should do more often. I never missed when my mother, God rest her, was alive. Nowadays . . . well, it gets away from a man."

"How long does it take to get to Portnoo?"

"A half hour should give us plenty of time."

"Good. I'd like to leave at nine-thirty."

After breakfast, with an hour before leaving Brian strolled down the main street. At the post office he mailed a letter to Maire and another, much longer, to Con. His wandering took him to the general store, where he was charmed by a small plastic knife loaded with a retractable blade. It looked like a fountain pen and it had a light in one end. He clipped it into

139

his jacket pocket. He considered his shiny Florsheims and bought black sneakers. He investigated the art gallery and bought a picture, which he arranged to pick up the next day. He made sure the owner of the gallery knew that he was going to visit the gardens at Portnoo.

"Pity it's not a better day." Jimmy put the car in gear and they backed out of the little yard behind the hotel. "It's only a short run to Portnoo through Maas, but I think there's no finer scenery in the whole country."

The road rolled on, passing isolated white cottages and small bogs with cut turf neatly stacked and drying. White sheep dotted the slopes under the lowering sky. When they got to Maas, Jimmy stopped so Brian could see Gweebarra Bay.

"In the old days the women from the Rosses knit wool socks for the gombeen man in Ballyglenfoyle. They used to wait on the other side for the tide to go out so they could wade across. Sometimes they had to wait for hours in the cold and rain. Sometimes they got caught on the turn and drowned. Sixteen hours' work to make a pair, and they got a penny for the work. Ah, those were the bad old days. Come on, man, or we'll be late getting to the gardens."

"Do you know how to find the place?" Brian pulled down his seat belt and gained an amused glance from Jimmy.

There was the blast of a horn as an arrogant CIE tour bus announced its approach. "Just follow the road hog. That must be the garden tour bus. They'll have come from Donegal Town."

Jimmy was right. The bus headed through gates to a Queen Anne house built of whitewashed local stone, its severe facade softened with climbing roses, and continued on to a car park discreetly hidden behind a tall privet hedge.

The crowd from the bus were mostly middle-aged, sensible, garden club types festooned with cameras. Their guide hustled them into a large reception area where a pleasant-looking woman of about forty-five was waiting.

"Welcome to Portnoo Gardens. I'm Margaret Garrity, and it's a great pleasure to have you here. If you'll find seats I'd like to show a short film about the history. . . ."

Brian chose a seat in the rear at the end of the row and examined the speaker with interest. He could see no resemblance to her brother. Several times she seemed to look directly at him. Could she possibly know who he was? When the film started she slipped out through a side door. He followed.

"Miss Garrity?"

"Yes?"

"I'm Brian Donodio. I met your brother Patrick in New York."

To his amazement, her eyes filled with tears. "You knew Patrick? Come in, come in." She led him across the parking space and into the house through a side door.

"This is my office. Sit down. I'll only be a moment, I have to tell one of my assistants to take over this tour."

There was a picture of Patrick Garrity on the desk. Next to it was a small vase with a single rose. Piled on top of a cabinet was a stack of glossy brochures about the Portnoo Gardens. He helped himself to a copy and sat down to await her return.

The brochure was informative. The gardens were a commercial success, he learned, their chief product being the Fianna line of perfumes and toiletries based on the carrageen moss that grew plentifully along the shore of the Gweebarra estuary.

He was still evaluating this information when a door in the wall opened.

"Won't you step this way into the lounge? We can talk better in here over a cup of tea."

He followed her through the door into an airy sitting room with a breathtaking view over the water. The words of admiration rising to his lips were never uttered. He heard a step on the hardwood floor, his nostrils were filled with the scent he was coming to loathe, and a crushing weight descended on the back of his head. Through shooting stars and rushing dark he heard a woman say, "Now we've got the bugger."

30

Deirdre touched up a small holiday on the door she was painting and gazed complacently at her handiwork. Maire was providing the decorator's touch, but the sweat equity was hers and Con's. She'd arrived bright and early to go on with the fixing up of the house, only to find Con out and no note. She'd wring his neck when he finally showed up.

Her musing was interrupted by the sound of a key in the lock.

"Anybody home?"

"In here. Where have you been?"

"Good morning, gorgeous. I like the white paint on your nose. It adds a touch of class. Listen, we have to talk . . ."

"Why? Don't tell me the furniture people have come up with another reason why they can't deliver the new couch when they promised."

He shook his head. "No, nothing like that. How long since your mother heard from your dad?"

"He called the day before yesterday. Why?"

"By the pricking of my thumbs. Has he called since he left Dublin?"

"No. Con, do you know something you're not telling me?"

"I had a call from Inspector McNulty in Dublin this morning, real early. You know, he's the guy I've been liaising with. All unofficial. He nearly bust a gut trying to get me to tell him everything while he told me nothing. Let's sit in the kitchen and have some coffee."

The first room tackled had been the kitchen. It gleamed in pristine, nuptial purity. Maire had chosen the antique gas stove as the focal point, sending it out to be cleaned and refinished in its original cream and pale green. Green and cream tiles formed the splashboard behind the sink and the theme was carried out in the green-sprigged cream curtains. The old cabinets had been stripped of nearly a century of paint to the original pine. Tall, double hung, many-paned windows overlooked the tiny back garden tended with care by Con's mother.

Deirdre looked around complacently. "I do like this room. I think I'd marry you just to get my hands on it." She plunked down at the table between the windows. "Out with it."

"Well, reading between the lines, I gather that Dublin has a sort of Irish clone of the Mafia operating. According to McNulty, the real point of the phony green cards is to get a hold on people who'll then be available for moving drugs in and out of Dublin and New York and, I guess, England and the Continent. They trap kids into it by telling them it's for the IRA and then pledging them to secrecy."

"Did this McNulty think that Dad was mixed up in a mess like that?"

"Let's say he was curious, and the Italian name didn't help. It seems that your dad took off yesterday for the north in the company of a Garda inspector who's a cousin to the woman who keeps the B and B on Clontarf Road where he's been staying."

Deirdre relaxed. "That's okay, then. He can't come to too much harm traveling around with a cop."

"Wrong. I gather whatever their equivalent is of Internal Affairs has been looking sideways at this guy for some time.

They're pretty sure he's tied in to this green card operation, but they have no hard evidence. McNulty said he had a couple of days off coming and the landlady says the two of them went north."

"Where did they go?"

"Where else? Ballyglenfoyle and Portnoo. They've alerted the local men."

"Let's go."

"Go where?"

"To Ireland, before Mother finds out. We both took a week's leave to get the apartment into shape, so we have time. Is your passport up to date?"

"Yes."

"The apartment can wait. You get the tickets while I go home and pack."

They barely made the flight. After Deirdre willed the plane safely off the ground and on its way, she turned to Con. "Do you have any idea where we start?"

"All roads lead to Ballyglenfoyle. That was Maureen's hometown and that's where Brian was headed, according to McNulty, who, by the way, is meeting us at Shannon. So just settle back and enjoy the flight."

"I hate flying"—Deirdre snuggled into a comfortable position against Con's shoulder—"but I don't mind it so much this time. I mean, once we got off the ground. For the first time ever I'm not trying to fly the plane." She turned and looked him in the eye. "Let me see your passport."

"No."

"Why not, for heaven's sake? I saw you staring at mine with that awful picture. Con, we're getting married in a few weeks. Don't you think it's time I found out your real name?"

"No."

"What are you going to do when we go for our license?"

"Lie."

"This is ridiculous."

She had never thought to see Con sheepish. Angry, yes. Mulish, yes. Ovine, never. He pulled out his passport and held it firmly away from her.

"I'll explain. My dad's hobby was military history. He was mad about victorious generals, unless they were English. My eldest brother is Hugh O'Neill Connolly. He's the lucky one. My other brother is Caesar Vespasian. My sisters are Scotia and Jeanne d'Arc Connolly. As for me"— he handed across the gold-stamped, blue booklet—"see for yourself."

Deirdre offered the supreme sacrifice. "Darling, if it means this much to you, just forget I asked. I won't look."

"Go ahead. You're right. You'll have to know in a couple of weeks." He turned his head and gazed stoically at the fat man snoring in the seat across the aisle.

She felt the giggles building even before she opened the fateful document. There it was, spelled out in living color for all the world to read: Hannibal Vercingetorix Connolly. She bit her lip trying to think of a suitable comment.

"Mrs. Hannibal Vercingetorix Connolly. I don't think we want a junior, do you?"

31

THERE WAS A pain in his head like a million sirens rising to full blast and then receding, only to rise again. He tried to lift his hands to the pain, only to discover them bound tightly behind his back. His legs were bound at the ankles. He opened his eyes carefully. He was lying on his side on a dusty floor. Dust from the floor triggered a fit of sneezing that intensified the pain in his head, and he passed out again. When he came to for the second time the pain was less. He rolled over cautiously and inched to a sitting position.

Where was Jimmy? By now the superintendent must have missed him. Well, he'd asked for it and now he had his answer. Blind panic began to build, shuddering up from deep inside his gut, setting his chest muscles shaking, driving tears to his eyes. His teeth clamped his lower lip until he tasted blood. He breathed deep, forcing himself to count slowly until he felt a fragile calm return. How long had he been unconscious? He flexed his wrists. They were tied with strong, thin twine that bit deep.

Through the window he heard the voices of the garden tour. That explained why they hadn't finished him off. They must be waiting until possible witnesses had left. Or maybe they wanted to question him before they killed him, for he had absolutely no doubt that his death was next on the agenda.

Trying not to make any noise, he inched his way to the wall and braced his shoulders. As a teenager he had fancied himself a magician and learned some of the simpler escapes. If he could slide his body through his bound hands so they were in front of him, he had a chance. But would his sixty-five-year-old body obey? It had to. God, his head hurt! He drew his knees up and cautiously tried to raise his rump. Red-hot pain cracked his shoulders and down his back, but his backside was firmly caught between his arms.

Cursing the rough tweed of his jacket, he raised himself again and pushed on another inch, and another, and another until he felt his wrists swing free beneath his cocked knees. It was a smaller struggle to force his bound feet through the circle of arms and rotate his shoulder muscles, which spasmed into agonizing cramps when the tension was released.

The bite of the twine had swollen his fingers into purple-black blood sausages, but the knife he had bought this morning was still in his breast pocket. Its plastic, push-button top must have deceived them into thinking it a pen. He fumbled it loose, but his fingers were too swollen to grip. The knife had a button in its side to release the blade. With infinite caution he raised it between his teeth, bit down, and the blade slid out. Footsteps sounded outside the door. The precious knife dropped and skittered across the floor. Brian closed his eyes and curled up to hide his arms as the door eased open.

"Still sleeping like a baby." Jimmy, the Garda inspector.

A woman's voice, quick and light—where had he heard it before? It wasn't Margaret Garrity. "He's moved."

Defensive. "Sure, what's the difference? He's trussed like a Christmas goose. He's not going anywhere."

"The eejits will be out of here in another hour, then we

can take care of him. We can't afford any traces to connect this place."

"And I can't afford any traces, either. What use will I be to you in prison?"

The door closed softly behind them. Until it had been withdrawn, he hadn't realized how much he had been pinning his hope on Jimmy, despite his suspicions. He slid painfully to the left to grope for the knife. In what seemed an age but was probably only seconds, his fingers touched the haft, but he could not get a grip. Finally he managed to raise it just enough to grip it again in his teeth. The nicks he sustained from the razor-sharp blade were nothing. Once it was positioned under the twine between his wrists it slid through like the proverbial hot knife through butter.

His legs were soon free, but agonizing minutes elapsed before circulation returned and he staggered to his feet to gaze out the window. From what the woman had said, he had an hour before the garden tour left.

The window overlooked the car park, where the tour bus and Jimmy's car were parked cheek to jowl. As he watched, Jimmy came out the back door and paused to wave to someone Brian couldn't see. When he drove away the bus stood empty and unguarded.

The window slid up easily to reveal a creeper up the back of the house within easy reach. Brian gulped. The vine would be a six-lane highway for superspy Richard Hannay or his cold war equivalent, James Bond. For a sixty-five-year-old retired history teacher who had been clobbered on the head and hog-tied it was just a trifle daunting. However, the door was out of the question. He'd be sure to be caught.

He rubbed his ankles, retrieved his knife, settled his clothes with as much decorum as possible, directed a brief prayer to whomever the patron saint of sturdy vines happened to be, took a deep breath, and swung his legs over the sill.

Nothing stirred below. The vine, thank God, was backed by a sturdy trellis. He cast a cautious downward glance and instantly wished he hadn't. His head went spinning out of control and bile rose to the back of his throat. Reason told him that the drop was about forty feet, his gut said it was a thousand. The dusty leaves pushed into his face and a misguided bee buzzed his head. Cautiously, testing each foothold, he crept earthward. Days, hours, minutes later, his reaching foot felt for the next hold. Nothing. Ground was solid under his feet. Ahead was the open door of the empty tour bus.

32

HE MADE IT. Inside, he scuttled on all fours up the aisle to the rear, where he crouched behind the last seat. With luck the bus would not be full and he could hide here until they got to the next stop. Mother of God, he was tired. He curled on his side and closed his eyes to ease his aching head.

The movement of the bus woke him up. Luck was with him; no one was riding in the back. The pain in his head had receded to a faint ache at the base of his skull. Up front, the chatter was of beds and borders, mulch and compost. Sensible talk from sensible people. The PA gave an apologetic hiccup and the talk died away.

"We will be stopping in Letterkenny for lunch for just one hour. Then we will proceed to Glenveagh. Letterkenny is the largest town in Donegal and is on the banks of the river Swilly. The name is derived from the Irish *Leitir Ceannain,* hillside of the O'Cannons."

Brian waited for the last gardener to leave the bus. When he was as presentable as possible he swung casually down the steps, waved to the driver, and uttered the quintessential Americanism before the astonished man could frame a query.

"Have a nice day."

What next? Fortunately, he still had his wallet. His wrists and ankles were throbbing from the cords, his headache was returning, his clothes were a mess, and he was ravenous.

Drugstore first. He looked up and down the street and was rewarded by a sign: MEDICAL HALL.

"Jaysus, what happened to you?" The druggist was a small man about his own age.

"I had a bit of an accident, what we Yanks call a fender bender. I need some painkiller, bandages, and something to put on my wrists." Brian held them out for inspection. "What do you advise?"

"A day in bed, by the look of you. Here, try this on your wrists. That never happened in a 'fender bender.' " He spread ointment on gauze squares and taped them handily over the blistering cord marks. "Anything else?"

"I hit my head; I need something for a headache."

"Let's take a look." Skillful fingers explored the lump rising behind Brian's ear. The man whipped out a small light and flashed it into his eyes.

"Your pupils are normal but you're going to have a hell of a goose egg behind your ear. Go in the back and wash up; I'll mix something to take the edge off the headache."

When Brian returned clean and somewhat refreshed, his Good Samaritan handed him a small cup of red liquid.

"It smells awful."

"And tastes worse, but it's good for what ails you. Take it all off in one gulp. If you sip, you'll never come back for the second taste."

His mouth puckered as if coated with alum and a line of heat streaked down to his toes.

"My God!" There was fire in his belly burning out the pain. He could feel it receding to a remembered ache, then even the shadow was gone. The druggist eyed him complacently.

"What the hell is this stuff?"

"A trade secret. And now, suppose you tell me what

really happened to you. That was no motor accident. You were tied up and coshed."

Brian considered. Should he tell this fellow? Would he believe him? Perhaps he was in league with the gang, who-ever they were. Maybe he'd put the man in jeopardy. On the other hand, the more people who knew about it, the safer he was. Look at it as an insurance policy.

While he pondered, the man put a sign up on the door and pulled down the shade. "No one will disturb us, I just put the "closed" sign up. Would you like to come upstairs and have a bite? The wife's away but I can give you a bowl of leftover stew and a cup of tea."

Brian's stomach made his decision. "I accept with plea-sure."

It was snug above the shop. Brian's host settled him at a scrubbed deal table that brought up a nostalgic yearning for Maire's kitchen. How he wished she were here to fuss over him.

"So what's it all about, then?" The stew was sending up a delicious smell. The first mouthful was ambrosial. Brian grabbed a piece of bread to sop gravy and spoke through a full mouth.

"My name's Donodio. Brian Donodio."

"Paddy Cannon."

"One of the Letterkenny Cannons?"

"There's lots of us around here, but all the glory left about seven hundred years ago. That's beside the point. You've been hit over the head, and I'm curious."

When Brian finished his story, Cannon shook his head. "I can see it all, except the part about Maggie Garrity. I've known Maggie since she was born, and if she's part of this, then I'm an Eskimo."

"But what about her brother Patrick?"

"Patrick Garrity was not her brother, God rest him. He was a cousin and a lot younger. She brought him up after the rest of his family was wiped out in the troubles in Belfast."

"Is Patrick dead?"

153

"Died in a motoring accident last month. His brakes failed and he went right down a steep slope. Car burst into flames and burned him to a crisp."

Finucane dead. Garrity dead. Brian was rapidly reevaluating his data. "Any chance his brakes could have been tampered with?"

"I don't suppose it even occurred to anyone. You should call the Garda."

"I've thought of that, but what am I to tell them? Everyone involved is a respectable citizen. Cousin Jimmy is one of their own, and you know how cops stick up for each other. If they call New York my son-in-law to be, Con Connolly, will tell them to get me on the first plane."

"I'd offer you a drink, but I don't think it would do your head much good. So what are you going to do?"

"Right now it's on the knees of the gods. I'd like to get the bastards dead to rights with witnesses whose word would count against theirs."

"Maybe Maggie would help."

"No. I know you're fond of her, but as far as I'm concerned, she's in this up to her neck."

"You're wrong. Oh, she's an IRA sympathizer. A lot of us are, and with good reason. She may have been fed a line of guff about Patrick working in the States for the movement. She'd believe that. And he may have been tricked into thinking all the dirty tricks were leading to a great blow at the Brits, then murdered when he found out differently or he was no further use to them."

"I don't think this has anything to do with the IRA, I told you that."

"And I agree. I'm going to call Maggie and get her over here."

"Will she come?"

"She'd better. Her mother, may she rest in peace, was my oldest sister."

33

THERE WAS A knock on the door. Cannon cocked his head at Brian. "That will be Maggie. Go in the next room; I want to hear what she has to say before she knows you're here."

"What's the big fuss?" Maggie burst through the door without ceremony. "Nothing's wrong with Breege or the boys, is there?"

"No, nothing like that. Breege is away in Dublin on her yearly shopping spree. She'll have me end my days a poor man. The boys are in France on some sort of church outing. Come in and sit down."

"I can't stay long. I'm glad you called, it gave me an excuse to get out of the house."

He glanced at her shrewdly. "Having problems, are you? Thought you might be. Come on, tell me about it."

"I hardly know where to begin."

"At the beginning. I'll just wet the tea while you're gathering your ammunition."

"Well, you know where my sympathies lie and you know that Patrick, God rest him, was working in the States for the IRA. At least I thought he was, but now I'm not so sure. These two, a man and a woman, came to the house yesterday."

Cannon poured. "How about a little drop of something in the tea? It will make the telling easier."

"Just a drop, then. I wish Breege was here, I could use her straight way of looking at things."

"You've always had a good head yourself."

"Well, I'm glad you called. I told them it would look funny if I didn't come when you said it was a family emergency." She shook her head. "Though how you knew something was wrong is beyond me. Anyroad, they told me this Yank would be coming this morning with another man, Jimmy Costigan. That he would say he was a friend of Patrick's, God rest him, but that it was a lie and that the organization wanted him for questioning."

"Then what happened?"

"As soon as he stepped through the door they whanged him on the head and tied him up. It just didn't seem right. I wanted to call the Garda, but Costigan said he was in the Garda and they wanted to catch this man dead to rights."

"So what made you think he was lying?"

"Use your loaf. The Garda doesn't go around whanging people on the head, they arrest them. And a real policeman wouldn't be working all open and above board with the organization. The other man was a mealy mouthed little devil in a suit that must have cost five hundred pounds if it cost a penny, like no organization man I've ever seen. And the girl with him was a smooth-talking piece all done up in tweeds and a twin-set. And get this, I'm sure she was wearing a wig."

"Well, that's no crime."

"Anyroad, I was glad when I saw the fellow climbing down the back of the house and getting away in the tour bus. I just sat tight and didn't say a word. When you called they didn't want me to come. But I told them if I didn't you'd be out to the house raising hell."

Brian decided it was time he made an appearance. He stuck his head around the door.

"Mind if I join the party?"

156

Her hand flew to her breast. "Mother of God, you scared the life out of me! Are you all right, then?"

"Fine, thanks to your keeping your mouth shut when you saw me climbing down. I don't think they're IRA either. Now, let me tell you the whole story . . ."

When he finished the tears were streaming down her face. "My poor little brother. I always called him that, you know, though he was really my cousin. I was only twenty when his two older brothers were killed in the troubles. His mother and father were taken in by the Brits and he never saw them again. I brought him up."

"There, Maggie"—Cannon put his arm around her— "that's long over."

"But Patrick scarcely cold," she sobbed, "and I'll bet Mr. Donodio is right, it was murder." She rounded on Brian with fiery eyes. "And he had nothing to do with Maureen Sullivan's death. My Patrick would have had no hand in murder."

This was not the time to argue. "Tell me, was Patrick good with computers?"

"Ah, he could make them sing. Set up the whole system for me at the gardens. The IRA never lost touch with him, felt they owed him something. Saw to it he had the best education Ireland could offer. He was a scholar at Trinity. So, Mr. Donodio, what do we do now?"

"With Paddy's permission, I'll spend the night here."

"You'll be very welcome. And you should rest that head for a day."

"Maggie, you go back to the house. Make up some sort of story about what Paddy wanted. Tomorrow I'll call you at Portnoo Gardens, and here's what we'll do. . . ."

157

It was six-thirty on a chilly morning when Con and Deirdre landed at Shannon. As soon as they were through passport control a tall, ruddy-faced man tapped Con on the shoulder.

"Sergeant Connolly?"

"Yes."

"I'm McNulty. There's a car outside."

"And this is Deirdre Donodio, Dr. Donodio's daughter and an agent of the INS."

"Have you any luggage?"

Con pointed at their carry-on bags. "Only what we're carrying."

"The roads will be clear at this hour. We should be in Ballyglenfoyle in about five hours."

He settled them in the car. "Your first visit to Ireland?"

"I've been before"—Deirdre chose the backseat and closed her eyes—"but Con hasn't."

McNulty rolled a humorous eye at Con, who was perching uneasily in the left-hand passenger seat. "Relax, man. We're used to driving this way. I nearly had a dozen heart attacks the first time I got in a car in the States. We'll let Miss Donodio catch a few winks and I'll point out the sights as we go along."

Con was not listening. He was thoroughly unnerved by the traffic sweeping down on the wrong side. Finally he gave a sheepish grin and settled back. Then he glanced at the speedometer and only saved himself from yelping when he realized that the speed was in kilometers instead of miles.

"I've been in touch with the lads in Ballyglenfoyle," McNulty continued. "As soon as we realized where they were headed, we alerted them to keep an eye out for the beauties. Sergeant Gildea picked them up as soon as they arrived. Of course, they didn't know who he was. I didn't want to tell you on the phone, but they lost track of Dr. Donodio yesterday morning. He went to seven o'clock Mass, had breakfast at the hotel. They took off again at half-past nine. It was our understanding they were visiting the Portnoo Gardens."

"What do they say at the gardens?"

"They say the only visitors yesterday were an American tour. But one of the girls who works there told our man that she saw a man answering Donodio's description drive up in a motor car with another man. He spoke to Miss Garrity and went into the house. That's the last she saw of him."

"Inspector McNulty . . ." Deirdre spoke up from the back seat.

"Call me Mike."

"Mike, I'm Deirdre, this is Con. We're strictly unofficial, and heaven knows, we don't want to interfere in any of your investigations, but he is my father. What about the hotel?"

"Costigan—that's what he's calling himself—checked them both out yesterday afternoon. I told Con here that we have our suspicions about Costigan, but you know how it is. I can't go into that now."

Being cops themselves, they knew just how it was, only they wished they didn't.

"Anyway, to cut a long story short, just for the moment we don't know where either of them is. While I was waiting for your plane the Shannon Garda heard from Dublin that Maureen Sullivan's dad went to the Garda station at Ballyglenfoyle with a very interesting letter from Dr. Donodio. We'll hear about it when we get there. I don't know the details. Their fax machine wasn't working."

They rounded a bend. Blocking the road was a flock of sheep being relentlessly chivied by a couple of businesslike collies. The shepherd gave a broad smile and wave but did nothing to hurry the process. McNulty sighed philosophically.

"Those are grand dogs he has there. Tell me——" He swiveled around to face the backseat. "Your father, now, he's an elderly man. Has he played detective before? Don't get offended now, but might he wander off, like, or imagine things?"

"If you knew my dad you wouldn't ask such a question. He's only sixty-five and as sharp as a knife. And he's never 'played detective,' as you put it, before. Tell him, Con."

The telling lasted through lunch at Tuam, a call in at the Garda post at Sligo to get the latest news, and all the way to Ballyglenfoyle.

35

BRIAN WISHED HE felt as confident as he looked. Twelve hours of solid sleep in Cannon's spare bedroom had done wonders for his head and other aches and pains, but there was a yawning vacuum where his stomach normally lived. A vacuum not eased by an enormous breakfast.

His appearance was wonderfully changed. An early morning foray by Cannon produced a kelly green sweatshirt that proclaimed to the world he was "Proud to Be Irish," a green-and-white baseball cap emblazoned with crossed Tricolor and Stars and Stripes, and trousers of unenviable cut in a horrid shade of red. Clip-on shades covered his own sedate horn-rims and the bottom touch was provided by yellow-and-blue sneakers.

Cannon stood back and admired his handiwork. "Ah, you're a sight to make maidens swoon."

"More likely to make them run for cover. I don't think I'll be recognized, do you?"

Cannon rummaged in a drawer. "I have the crowning touch for you." He produced a small radio with earphones.

"No. I've never walked down the street like a zombie, and I refuse to start now."

"This has a tape recorder in it. Slip it in your pocket and you can get a record of everything the buggers say."

"Ah, wise as the serpent and simple as the dove, that's me. Thanks, Paddy." A quick glance at his watch told him the time was now. "We have to be going."

Downstairs, Cannon put a sign on the door: GONE FISHING. Brian's eyebrows rose. "Will your customers accept that?"

"They'll have to, won't they? I read a book years ago about a Yank who put up that sign whenever he wanted to get out of the office. I've been dying to try it. Now's my chance. Come on, now. My motorcar is just around the back."

Just before they reached Ballyglenfoyle, Cannon pulled his little Morris Minor off the road into a lay-by to unstrap a battered bike from the rack on top.

"This is as close as I dare come. Go straight ahead to the turn and I'll follow easy like. I've strapped a pair of rubber boots to the carrier. You'll need them in the bog. I don't think we've been spotted and I doubt if your own mother would recognize you, but we'd best be careful."

Brian temporized. It was twenty years since he had ridden a bike and morning's cold reality was quenching the boasts of the night before.

"You'll call Maggie as soon as you get to the hotel?"

"I will, that. And I know just what to tell her."

"And you'll meet me as soon as she calls you back?"

"Honest to God, Donodio, if I didn't know you were keen as mustard for this thing I'd think you were procrastinating."

"And you'd be right. Well, here goes nothing."

He mounted his rusty steed and yawed magnificently. For a sickening moment he thought he would fall off the other side. Then he felt the balance. His knees protested as they conformed to a long-forgotten motion, the roadway whizzed beneath his wheels; he was off.

Outside the post office he stopped to telephone Dualta Sullivan.

"It's all set. Just as soon as they knock off work at the bog. . . . Sure, I'm okay. You were just doing as we agreed when you gave the Garda the envelope. . . . Well, it can't be helped. . . . I'm no hero, I hope they do turn up." He hung up the receiver thoughtfully.

Around the corner and up the main street he sped. Eyes turned to follow his progress and many a head shook in wonder at the crazy Yank. At the corner by the Garda station the road branched off up the glen. Sergeant Gildea, who had met him at the hotel and lost him in Portnoo, watched him pedal away. Gildea did not raise the alarm. As Paddy Cannon had said, even his own mother would not have recognized him.

36

WITH PLENTY OF time in hand, Brian pedaled slowly out the glen road. His legs were not protesting. He blessed Maire and the exercise program she had dogged him into. The sky overhead was a bright, clear blue dotted here and there with small fleecy clouds. In the fields on each side of the road the farmers were taking advantage of the weather to bring in the hay. Higher up the sides of the glen the lime-washed stone houses looked down benevolently on the harvesting. Cows in the upper pastures grazed and ruminated, thinking whatever thoughts cows think. Perhaps of milk, and calves, and rigorously controlled encounters with great red and black bulls. Or maybe the sad insults modern breeding practices afford to nature.

He dismounted to sit on a low stone wall and closed his eyes. The clans had marched and fought over these hills and glens. First against each other, with few deaths and cattle as the victor's prize. Later the struggle had been against the foreigner and the stakes death, enslavement, and ruin as a people. The constant earth had absorbed it all and still gave freely of her bounty.

Now there was a new enemy who cunningly hid behind

the death throes of the seven-hundred-year struggle with England. Was he the only one who saw it? Did he have to stand alone like Cu Chulainn of old and face down Banba's newest enemy?

He blushed at the grandiose thought and opened his eyes. "Of all the vainglorious, ridiculous, swell-headed romancers, you take the biscuit," he muttered to himself.

A youngster driving a cow down the road stopped with a worried frown.

"Are you all right, then? It's terrible hot out here in the sun."

Now he was really embarrassed. "I'm fine, thanks." He swung his leg over the bicycle.

"If you're thirsty, there's water up ahead piped out to the side of the bridge. Terrible day for riding a bike." He tickled the cow's rump with a switch and went on.

Five minutes ride brought him to the bridge and the promised drink. Clear, cold water flowed from a pipe into a stone basin. Crude letters chipped in the rock above admonished: "Jesus said, 'I thirst.' Drink and think of Him."

Half an hour further on he was in sight of his objective. He had planned to arrive well ahead of the proposed rendezvous so that he could check that his arrangements were in place, but they had outsmarted him. Two people already were waiting on top of the flat capstone of the dolmen at the edge of the bog. He pulled on the rubber boots and started out.

37

"So I was right, you two are behind all this. It was your perfume that finally tipped me off. When you danced with me that first night at the center. Remember?"

The sun was sliding to the west over the bog where the workers of the Bord na Mona were still going about their business, pausing every now and then to cast a curious glance at the three perched on top of the dolmen. Brian stretched his long legs in their knee-high rubber boots out in front of him and gazed mildly about, trying to give the impression that it took more than a gun pointing at his belly to unnerve him.

"Tell me about it." He slipped his hand into his pocket to be sure the switch on the little recorder was on.

"Don't tell him a thing, Dad. Why don't you just shoot him and be done with it? It'll be his own fault, the bloody, interfering bastard. I should have finished him at the gardens instead of just knocking him out." The girl's eyes were little holes of hate, her words spitting out between tense lips.

"I don't think he can do that just yet, Melly, if I may call you that and if that is your real name, which I doubt. Someone might notice."

The conventionally dressed young woman in well-cut tweeds and green Wellies was a far cry from the punk rocker he had first known in New York. "Is that a wig you're wearing? I like it much better than the shaved head you sported the last time I saw you. Very lifelike."

His gaze shifted to the man. "We have nothing to do but sit here and talk while I'm waiting to be shot. I thought it a little too convenient that you just happened to sit next to me on the plane, and I still don't know how you managed it. I'll even give you a piece of advice. Next time don't wear a five-hundred-dollar suit in tourist class. It makes a man wonder."

Turlough McSwiggan shifted his weight to his other buttock but kept the gun pointed steadily at Brian's navel. "That was a mistake. The whole scheme was going like silk until you interfered."

"Was it? I'd have thought it turned sour when Monica was murdered."

"I had nothing to do with that."

"No?" Brian's eyes slipped marginally sideways to the backhoe parked beside the rock, its serrated scoop raised. "Do you think the brakes are secure on that monster? If it slipped it could bash in all three of us."

McSwiggan chuckled with genuine amusement. "You can't take me in that way. It's safe enough. The fellows who work the bog are careful."

"If you say so. So Monica wasn't your doing. Okay, how about Maureen?"

"That was another mistake. I hate killing. I could have had you finished off at St. Anne's Garden, but I told the man just to warn you. I let my better nature get in the way of business. I won't be so foolish this time."

"Melly, what's your real name?"

"That's no concern of yours."

"Don't be rude, dear. Dr. Donodio, I do apologize, she's been under a terrible strain. May I present Mary Imelda McSwiggan, my daughter and the real brains of our enterprise."

167

"Dad, will you shut up! How do we know he doesn't have something up his sleeve?" She glanced at the sun and at the men who were packing up their tools and closing down their machines for the night. "Not long now, and I'll be glad to see the back of him."

"So, how about it, Mary Imelda? Was it you who stabbed Maureen, or was it that gutless wonder Patrick Garrity?"

To his surprise, she answered. "You're right about Patrick, calling him a gutless wonder. He had the brains and the looks, and he could charm the birds off the trees, but he had no bottom. Oh, I had great plans for Patrick. Then, that night up at Maureen's apartment, I was the one who had to stab her because she knew too much. The computers and all. Patrick went as soft as a grape. Said he'd known her since she was a little girl and couldn't leave her like that."

"So it was he who laid her out with the rosary and all? I wonder that you let him. The police would probably have taken it for a random killing but for that. Some junkie who broke in thinking the place was empty."

"He sneaked back later and did that. That was when I decided he was no more use to us." Her hands clenched together hard so the knuckles stood out like white knobs, and an ugly red suffused her face. "And don't think it didn't hurt, because it did. We were about to pack it in and retire with more money than you could dream of and all the machinery in place to keep it coming in without ever a trace back to us."

"Now, Melly . . . ," McSwiggan interrupted. The gun never wavered and he kept his eyes glued on Brian.

"Don't 'now Melly' me, you softheaded git. You wanted it as much as I did. The house in the country and the suite at the Shelbourne, the box at the horse show with our own horses taking prizes and you swanking around in a top hat. And me on Patrick's arm with the best of them. Not bad for a couple of wankers from the Falls Road." Her voice rose to a high-pitched whine. "And we'd have had it all, if it wasn't for this . . ." She uttered an unspeakable obscenity.

"We all have our dreams. Too bad yours passed through the gates of ivory," Brian remarked.

"Shut up. You, with your superior smirk and your classical allusions that you think the rest of us are too dumb to catch. My dream was through the gates of horn until you came along."

"Touché. But why did you have to get rid of Patrick? I'm assuming that the brakes on his car were sabotaged."

"Because, would you believe it, the fool really believed that this was all for dear old Ireland."

Brian could not conceal his revulsion. "How about Finucane and Monica and God knows how many others? Did they all think the same?"

It was all coming out now. She was sure he would be dead soon and she could not resist an audience. A cold finger in his vitals told him she might be right.

"Dead right, they did. And all our couriers not knowing each other and dead afraid of the immigration. It's a beautiful scheme and I'm not going to let it go."

Brian glanced at his watch. Fifteen minutes and the peat workers would be through. He had enough on the tape to hang the two of them. All he had to do was spin this out.

"It's all over, Melly. The INS and the Garda are checking the computers now; they'll be able to track down everyone. Sooner or later someone will give you two away. If I found the two of you, don't you think someone else will? Besides, I wrote down everything I've figured out and mailed it all to Sergeant Connolly this morning."

"It's too late for you," McSwiggan remarked. "Your friend Sullivan isn't hiding in that backhoe listening to every word. He's been unavoidably detained. We took care of Cannon, too."

So he'd outsmarted himself again. Gibbering black panic trembled in his gut. He fought it down and managed to smile. "And Maggie?"

"Is one of us. She saw you climb down and hide in the bus. The trippers started coming back before she could get

169

hold of me to drag you out. One of our fellows followed and we knew when Cannon called that it must be about you."

There were still a few workers on the far side of the bog. It was now or never; he had to make his move. He rose abruptly. Before the two could react, his foot flashed out to catch McSwiggan under the chin, slamming his head back with a satisfying thwack. The next minute he was over the side of the dolmen and racing for the trees.

Shouts and cursing pursued him, and through his panic he was relieved to hear McSwiggan's deep tones. He really hadn't wanted to kill the fellow. Now he had to get to the Garda station with his tape.

38

IT WAS LATE when Con and Deirdre arrived in Ballyglenfoyle with a thoroughly disgruntled Inspector McNulty. The flock of sheep had been a minor delay. More serious had been a jackknifed tractor trailer completely blocking the road. Common decency had forced them to give what aid they could to the critically injured driver until the professionals arrived. And there was another agonizing wait while the wrecking crews cleared the road; then McNulty had to make a statement at the local station.

They found the Ballyglenfoyle gardai buzzing with excitement. Mr. and Mrs Sullivan, bound and gagged in their own kitchen, had been found by their youngest son when he came home from an after school hurley match in the next town. And if that wasn't enough excitement for one day, Paddy Cannon from Letterkenny had been set upon out on the Glen Road, hit on the head, and left tied up and gagged behind the wall of the old cemetery. Mrs. Brosnahan from up the glen had found him while chasing a wandering hen. He was over at the doctor's house now, getting his head patched up. They were trying to sort out their stories, and no one had much time for the three arrivals from Dublin. They were ushered into a side room to wait their turn.

Inspector McNulty was not a man who took kindly to waiting. "You two stay here for a few minutes while I go and light a few fires. They'll take it more kindly from me than from you. I'm sure you understand."

"I understand, but hurry," was Con's rejoinder. "If you came to our side, I could stir up a Staten Island precinct faster than you."

"Precisely."

Deirdre was almost, not quite, in tears. "Why did we ever let him come? Dammit, Con, I knew he was up to something."

"And how could you have stopped him, short of locking him up? He's a full-grown, competent adult. Stop blaming yourself. Sometimes I wonder about 'competent,' though."

McNulty returned with a thin middle-aged man in worn tweeds.

"This is Sergeant Gildea. He was keeping an eye on your father. I'd like you to hear his story."

"No time for stories." Gildea was a man of few words. "From what we've heard from Sullivan and Cannon, we should find them at the bog where they cut the peat. That's where your father set up the meeting, on top of a bloody great dolmen. Sullivan was supposed to hide in his machine and be a witness, but they got to him first. A bunch of loonies if you ask me—excuse me, Miss Donodio—playing detective like this. The cars are waiting. Sergeant Connolly, we'd be glad to have you come along. I saw Dr. Donodio this afternoon all dressed up like everyone's dream of a comic Yank; he was wobbling along up the Glen Road on an old bicycle. I thought he looked familiar, but I couldn't place him. He was nothing like the man I met over in the hotel."

"I'm coming too."

"It's no place for women."

"I think he's right, darling. Not because you're a woman, but because he's your father. It's like a doctor treating his own family."

"Con, I'm not arguing. I'm coming. I'm a trained police

172

officer, just the same as you. If it was your father, you'd be there."

Con shrugged. "Come on, then. Remember, we're only observers."

Outside, someone threw rubber boots at them. "You'll need these for the bog. I hope they fit. That car over there, in with the dogs. Don't worry, they're well trained."

"Dogs?"

"We may not need them, but if we do, it's handy to have them along."

Deirdre absorbed this information in silence. The picture in her mind was a vague mélange of quicksand, sinkholes, sucking mud pulling her father down, down, while bloodhounds bayed and led the searchers to a spot where there was nothing to see but a still surface hiding its dreadful secret.

The garda driving was a cheerful young man. "I'm the dog handler. The dignified fella is MacTavish, the affectionate one is Bran. He'll be all over you if you let him."

Deirdre found this out for herself. Bran, a sad-eyed bloodhound with outsized paws and ears that swept low, fancied himself a lap dog. He rested his head and front paws on her knees while she scratched behind his ears. MacTavish sat bolt upright on the seat next to her, discouraging familiarity with his aloof posture and steady, low growl.

Con sat quietly in the front seat while Deirdre inwardly fumed. I'm in the back because I'm a woman, and I can't say a word. Please, God, don't let anything happen to Dad. I'll be good. She realized that she was slipping back to childhood and shook herself, surprised to find that slow tears were running down her cheeks.

Silence hung over the bog. Mechanical diggers, bulldozers and backhoes stood in quiet ranks on the side. The last of the workers had gone except for the night watchman brewing tea in his shack.

"What's it all about, then?" The watchman emerged as the first of the police cars pulled in.

Sergeant Gildea was first out. "Seen anyone hanging around?"

"Not I. Jimmy Corcoran told me there were three people sitting on top of the big rock earlier. He was going to go over and chase them away before he left, but when he looked they had left already. Would they be who you're after?"

"Perhaps. You mean they were sitting on top of the dolmen?"

"Where else is there to sit?"

"Thanks." He raised his voice. "We're going to start at the dolmen. Aidan says three people were seated on it earlier. Drive round and get the dogs ready."

"That's Dad's bag and that's his jacket," Deirdre whispered to Con as the dog handler gave MacTavish and Bran a good sniff. "Where did they get them?"

MacTavish was true to his temperament. He was still checking out the dolmen when Bran gave tongue and pulled his handler to the fringe of trees rimming the bog. Con and Deirdre went stumbling after.

39

THE LIGHT WAS dim beneath the trees. Brian looked frantically around for a hiding place, but this was no natural woodland. This was man-planted, with straight-ruled ranks of pines and no friendly undergrowth where a fugitive could go to ground. A windbreak for the bog workers. Already he could glimpse the open country beyond the trees.

He broke into the open, legs still pumping at an amazing rate as his system poured out adrenaline. His mind chugged on in a rhythm of its own. First he had to get rid of his ridiculous green sweatshirt. Its screaming color targeted him for pursuers as surely as a spotlight.

There was a small rise ahead of him. He crested it in one leap and rolled down on the far side, wiggling out of his sweatshirt as soon as he hit dirt, cramming it and his unspeakable baseball cap behind a bush. He raised his head cautiously above the lip of the rise just in time to see Melly and McSwiggan burst out of the trees.

If he stayed where he was they'd have him in a couple of minutes. To his right the rise petered out in a few yards. To his left it rose higher until it met an unpaved road, really only a track, going up the side of the hill. Next to the track was a ditch.

He inched left on his belly. When the rise above grew tall enough he ran doubled over until he reached the ditch, which was filled with clear, amber-brown peat water running off the bog. Behind he could still hear them running back and forth. Soon they would figure out where he must have gone. He didn't dare lie down in the water for fear of ruining his precious tape.

For now it was climbing, slow foot by foot, bent double, forgetting what was behind. The pain in his back was excruciating. Still, it's remarkable how much fortitude is engendered by the momentary expectation of a bullet in the back. Ahead a willow leaned over the bank, its low branches and long leaves reaching to the edge of the water.

"Here's his shirt and cap." Melly's voice cut through the still air. "This way." They'd see him in a minute. He slipped beneath the sheltering leaves.

Behind the green tent was a hollow scooped into the bank, the entrance nearly concealed by a large clump of bracken. He slipped behind the ferns and pulled the growth over to hide the edges of the hollow. Just in time. McSwiggan's voice sounded not two feet from where he had gone to earth.

"God knows where the bugger's gone. There's nowhere back here for anyone to hide."

"What do we do now?"

"What does the cat do when the mouse vanishes?"

"You and your bloody riddles."

"He watches. Donodio has gone to earth somewhere. Sooner or later he has to make a break." Wellingtoned feet splashed away through the ditch.

Brian's grip on the fronds relaxed, allowing dim light to filter into the hole. He had stumbled upon some child's secret hideout. In it was a trowel, a tin box of cookies, and other treasures he was careful not to disturb. The hollow was damp, but snug withal. He stashed the tape recorder inside the box and hid it in a hollow he scooped in the dirt, then lay down to listen and wait for darkness. Listening slipped into

176

uneasy slumber, punctuated by dreams of barking dogs and shouting men.

He was jarred out of sleep by a calamitous cramp in his left leg. It was full night, lit by silver beams from a gibbous moon that penetrated fitfully through the willow leaves. He dared a quick peep through the leaves. Outside his circle of quiet the night was awake with soft rustles and squeaks. More to the point, a broad swath of light spilled down the hillside from a cabin at the top. A cabin he had not noticed in the haste of his flight. Beyond the belt of pine he could hear the belling of the dogs that had echoed in his dreams. Had McSwiggan and Melly called on their accomplices to track him down with dogs? He shuddered with the atavistic fear of feral attack. There was no sound in his immediate vicinity, but caution was still in order. Once he had stamped and kicked out his cramp he did not take to the track, he crept the rest of the way to the house through the ditch and knocked on the door.

"The door is on the latch. Come in," quavered an ancient voice.

She was ninety if she was a day, tiny and bent, her hair wisping in white locks across her skull, her face a crosshatch of wrinkles and her mouth a toothless hole. From under shaggy brows a pair of faded blue eyes stared up at him. Brian remembered his manners.

"God bless all here."

"And His blessing on you, stranger." One eye closed in a wink. "Are you on the run?"

"On the run?" he repeated stupidly.

"Lord save us, the divils have addled him entirely. Are the Black and Tans after you?"

"They are." Good Lord, he thought, she's living in the past. I'll have to go along with it. "May I stay here for a while?"

"And welcome. They'll not get you like they did my man.

Not while Bridget O'Toole has life in her body. Here, sit next to the fire and I'll have a bite for you in just a moment." Glowing peat in the iron fireplace sent out a welcome glow. Brian slumped in an old wooden armchair that would have brought a gleam to Maire's eyes, and looked around. Against one wall was a deal dresser showing off an astonishing array of delft pottery. Against the other a long settle piled with cushions took the place of a couch. Over it a picture of Pope Pius XI imparted the papal blessing. Hidden in the shadows was an ancient refrigerator. She took out a covered plastic dish.

"I have some lovely stew left over and it will only take a minute to heat."

Brian was half dozing in the fire warmth. He sat up straight when she muttered, "Now, I'll put it in the wee machine," and a succession of beeps announced that his stew was heating in a microwave.

"I'm surprised you have one of those all the way out here."

"Lovely, isn't it? Ethne, my granddaughter, brought it to me from Dublin last summer. Now, lad, tell me what trouble you're in. You're a Yank, aren't you? My man was a Yank. Came over here to help and he got six feet of earth for his pains."

"Well, I . . ."

There was thunderous knocking on the door.

"They're here! Quick, into the chest with you. I'll try to hold them off. If I can't, you'll find what you need in there."

Without waiting for his answer she flung back the lid of a huge, half-filled box. He crammed himself down on an assortment of mysterious knobby objects and listened. It was Turlough McSwiggan, oozing oily charm.

"Good evening, madam. I'm from the Garda and this is Ban Garda Costello."

Why, the dirty rat . . . Brian nearly choked with indignation, but all the time he was feeling beneath him. What an interesting shape . . .

"We're hunting for a dangerous escaped prisoner. He's about six feet, thinning hair, horn-rimmed glasses. When last seen he was wearing red pants and running shoes. May we come in?"

"You may not!"

Oh, bless you, Bridget. Brian was still feeling carefully beneath him. He knew what the thing was. Dammit, why wouldn't his brain work?

"I think you're the Black and Tans. You look like Black and Tans to me."

"I can see you're a woman to be trusted." Clever Turlough. He was changing his tune. "I wouldn't tell everyone this, but the truth is . . ."

Brian felt his heart sink. The bastard was speaking Irish and so was Melly.

He eased the shape out from under and ran loving fingers over it. Now he knew—it was an old over-under, by the feel of it the same as his father had years ago. He·knew its secrets well.

They were speaking English again. "He's a dangerous man, and if we don't catch him, a lot of good men may die. You wouldn't want to have that on your soul, would you now?" He added with intentional brutality, "And you so close to meeting your Maker."

Bridget had spirit. "It's because I'm so close to the end that I won't soil my soul by giving in to the likes of you. God never closes one door but He opens another. Besides, what makes you think I've seen the Yank?"

"And how did you know he's a Yank, if you haven't seen him? Let's stop wasting time. We've been watching. We saw you let him in a few minutes ago. We're going to search. You can make it easy on yourself by telling us where he is, or we can tie you up and let you watch."

Now. Brian cracked the lid. They had their backs to the chest and were lashing Bridget to a chair while she struggled feebly.

"You miserable *peist*—" Her protest was cut short by the

179

impact of flesh on flesh. Something inside Brian snapped. No one was going to beat up on an ancient lady while he cowered inside a box. He crashed the lid back against the wall with a mighty thwack as he rose to cover them with the venerable shotgun. He hoped to hell it was loaded, and he prayed that he wouldn't have to find out the hard way.

"That's not necessary, McSwiggan. Let her go."

McSwiggan gave the antique in Brian's hand a scornful glance. "If you think you can frighten me with that popgun, you're mistaken. It probably doesn't even shoot." His hand groped under his jacket.

It was the moment of truth. He swung the old gun in a smooth arc to the window and pulled the trigger.

The explosion was deafening, flame leaped from the muzzle, and the window disappeared.

"Sorry about that, Bridget. I'll make good the damage." He swung the gun back. "Now, I'm going to march the two of you—" He never finished the sentence. Outside, the night was filled with the barking of dogs. A voice through a loud-speaker trumpeted, "This is the Garda and we have men all about the cabin. Come out with your hands in the air."

"You heard the man. Do as he says. First, though, take your gun from your holster and drop it nice and easy on the floor."

"The hell with you, you bastard," McSwiggan was raging past all reason. "You don't have the guts to use that shotgun. If they're getting me, I'll make damn sure I get you first." His hand reached again under his jacket.

Bridget was still helpless in the chair. Melly was crouched in a corner, her eyes spitting hate. Even as his finger closed on the trigger a montage flashed in his head: Maureen's face covered with flies, her body laid out on the couch with a knife through her heart; Monica's pathetic closed coffin con-taining nothing but decayed, animal-chewed flesh. Finu-cane, slumped over his desk; and Garrity a scorched lump of cooked meat in a ditch. All to be laid at the door of this oily-tongued lickspittle and his unspeakable daughter.

The recoil hurled him back and he gazed with disbelief at the red ruin of McSwiggan's back. There was a crash as the door gave way and the room was filled with uniformed men.

"Daddy, Daddy, are you all right?" Deirdre threw herself into his arms.

"Let me take that." Con relieved him of the antique gun.

"Be careful, it's loaded. Deirdre, Con, what the hell are you two doing here?"

Later that night, after statements were taken and sworn to, the prisoners booked, lawyers called, and lines burned up between Ballyglenfoyle and Dublin Castle, Brian, Deirdre, Con, and Bridget were guests of the Garda at a celebration. A private room at the hotel was set aside for the occasion. After all of the speeches were made and toasts were drunk, Sergeant Gildea approached the three Yanks.

"We've been able to tie up some more loose ends. Jimmy Costigan, not the name his mother gave him, is a real superintendent, I'm ashamed to say. It was he who took a pot shot at you at Tara. He's in custody. His cousin Mrs. Molloy was just a dupe. He fed her some folderol about a secret mission when she told him you were coming over to stay. Margaret Garrity has been arrested and her uncle, Pat Cannon, a decent man, still cannot believe it of her. All in all, a very satisfactory night's work. Now"——he took a reviving swig from his glass——"what are your plans? Are you going to take a few days' holiday?"

Deirdre was firm. "No. We have an apartment to paint and we'll have lost two workdays by the time we get home. We have to be ready for the wedding in three weeks." She hugged Brian. "This one has promised to have the garden in tip-top shape for the reception, so he'd better come with us. We're taking the first plane out of here."

"And remember," Con added, "when you get finished with Melly and her gang of thieves, that we want them in New York on murder one."

"To say nothing of computer crimes," added Deirdre.

"And drug smuggling," contributed Brian.

Sergeant Gildea put a finger alongside his nose and winked at Con. "You're welcome to them, if they're still around to be sentenced. I do have one word of advice for you, Dr. Donodio. Next time leave it to the professionals."

"There won't be a next time." Deirdre grabbed hold of his arm. "I'll see to that."

"Time will tell," Brian answered.

The New York Times, Sunday, September 1:

Deirdre MacMorrough Donodio, the daughter of Dr. and Mrs. Brian MacMorrough Donodio of Woodside, was married to Mr. H. V. Connolly of Manhattan on Saturday, August 31. The nuptial mass was celebrated by Rt. Rev. Msgr. Phelim O'Toole in St. Enda of Aran's church in Woodside, followed by a garden reception at the Donodios' residence in Woodside. Mr. Connolly, the son of the late Capt. Manus Connolly of the New York City Police Department and Mrs. Ingrid Connolly of Manhattan, is a sergeant with the New York City Police Department and a graduate of Fordham University. Ms. Donodio, a graduate of Mt. St. Vincent, is a former special agent with the Immigration and Naturalization Service. Following a wedding trip to Italy, the couple will reside in Manhattan. Ms. Donodio will retain her maiden name.

Special to the *Donegal Democrat:*

Saturday, August 31, was a great day in Woodside, New York, when Deirdre MacMorrough Donodio and Sergeant

H. V. "Con" Connolly of the New York City Police Department were joined in holy matrimony. The deed was accomplished in the Church of St. Enda of Aran in Woodside, where the happy couple were piped down the aisle by pipers from the police department's Emerald Society. The nuptial mass was offered by Rt. Rev. Msgr. Phelim O'Toole, who bestowed the Papal Blessing. The bride was escorted down the aisle by her father, Dr. Brian MacMorrough Donodio, who is well known in Ballyglenfoyle and famous throughout Ireland as the man who brought an infamous gang of criminals to justice, and her mother, Maire MacPherson Donodio, who is very active in the immigration reform movement. The bride's only attendant was her sister, Maria Donodio Hanley. Doing the honors for the groom was his brother, Hugh O'Neill Connolly. The reception was held in the magnificent and famous gardens of the Donodio home in Woodside, where the wine flowed like buttermilk and the pipers, an Italian band, and a regular dance band were hard put to keep up with the merriment. Following a wedding trip to Italy, Mr. and Mrs. Connolly will make their headquarters in Manhattan, but we hope they will be frequent visitors to Donegal where every door is on the latch for them.

The *Irish Times,* Monday, September 2:

Mary Imelda McSwiggan was sentenced to life imprisonment today after being found guilty of the murder of Patrick Garrity of Donegal. She was also found guilty on lesser charges of drug smuggling and dealing, computer piracy, tax evasion, and interfering in the internal affairs of another sovereign country (USA).

In the United States there are outstanding warrants on her for three known murders (including Ban Garda Maureen Sullivan), computer piracy, drug smuggling, and assisting illegal entry into the country.

The verdict will be appealed.